THE BULLS OF COYANOSA

When the parish priest sought to make money for the restoration of his mission, he bought longhorn cows but did not alter the bull calves, and the sky fell on him. The crisis was serious, but before a decision was made about his bulls, Coyanosa was attacked by a large band of renegades. Constable Elrey Austin had reason to fear widespread destruction, and only the bulls of Coyanosa could save the town from impending disaster.

RAY KELLY

THE BULLS
OF
COYANOSA

Complete and Unabridged

LINFORD
Leicester

First published in Great Britain in 1992 by
Robert Hale Limited
London

First Linford Edition
published 2000
by arrangement with
Robert Hale Limited
London

British Library CIP Data

Kelly, Ray
    The bulls of Coyanosa.—Large print ed.—
Linford western library
1. Western stories
2. Large type books
I. Title
823.9'14 [F]

ISBN 0–7089–5666–1

Published by
F. A. Thorpe (Publishing)
Anstey, Leicestershire

Set by Words & Graphics Ltd.
Anstey, Leicestershire
Printed and bound in Great Britain by
T. J. International Ltd., Padstow, Cornwall

This book is printed on acid-free paper

1

A Cause of Trouble

It was said of Father Cross his mistake was to engage in the breeding of bulls for livestock trade in what amounted to the holy man's desperate effort to save Mission San Angelo when every knowledgeable person in the Middle Domain of New Mexico Territory knew from experience that stockmen from the north, as well as to the east in Texas and to the west, what would sixty-five years after the Holy Father's passing be known as the Territory of Arizona, had passed beyond using razorback bulls with six-seven foot horn spans and mottled slab-sided rib cages.

Cattlemen bought up-graded, short legged, measly-horned red backed cattle with short legs and white faces, whose barrel-shapes ensured a beefier variety of cattle.

Feliciano Cortez and Dodge Plummer, range cattlemen of experience, large holdings and solid substance, shook their heads.

For one thing they did not want razorback bulls on the range, which was unfenced and open in all directions for hundreds of miles, land over which they and others ran great amounts of up-bred cows with high grade Hereford bulls.

They were beef cattlemen, like most of the other ranchers in the Coyanosa country, their livelihood depended upon solid-bodied meat animals. One razorback bull could cover forty cows. Next calving time the calves of such unions were leggy, orry-eyed, grew tall, were wicked horned, could run like deer and would fight a buzz saw.

They were not only difficult to handle in comparison to redbacks, they could also out run some very good horses, foraged where they pleased, chased people on foot, sometimes even those on horseback, and, in short, had been useful once, in the beginning when wolves and pumas systematically thinned herds, but with predator devastation largely eliminated, the business of raising cattle had become a very practical business of minimal handling of relatively docile animals who could not out run a horse and whose measly horns were practically harmless. No cowman wanted to go back, and that, it was emphatically stated, was exactly what Father Cross was trying to do by buying cheap razorbacks, raising the bull calves without altering them, and running his troublesome longhorns on open range, which did not really belong to anyone, but which had been the realm of local stockmen for many years, men whose interests were identical, whose goals and ambitions were identical, and holy man or not, they had no intention of tolerating longhorn bulls among their up-bred whitefaced cows.

It was not the only problem facing people in the Coyanosa country, but as time passed and more and more comparatively docile, stumpy-legged and barrel-bodied Hereford cows came in after calving with long legged wild razorback calves at their sides, it became a problem of magnitude to all the threatened cattlemen, and that included some ranchers a hundred miles from Coyanosa who had no idea where those longhorn bulls came from, they simply knew the quality of their saleable two-year-olds was in jeopardy; cattle buyers did not want anything on the hoof that grew tall, remained slab-sided all their lives, and the handling of which was at times next to impossible.

In consequence of Father Cross's desperate attempt to alleviate the chronic financial difficulties of his San Angelo Mission, which had been embarked upon with the innocence of a priest whose intentions had been of the best, came in time to represent a genuine threat to the careful and systematic inauguration of raising quality beef-cattle, which in fact was an undertaking requiring many years — in human terms a full generation — to breed out the longhorn blood and replace it with Hereford blood.

No one would go back to the kind of cattle their fathers had raised; there was no longer any need for animals who could take care of themselves against any predator. And there was another factor, rarely discussed because it reflected against the present generation of riders: The oldtimers had developed an excellent system for working their longhorns. For the most part they were gone now, and along with their passing went the exuberant, reckless, very dangerous practices they had perfected, and of which their sons and grandsons had not the least idea, and this, in the view of oldtimers in the Coyanosa country was very funny. It was also something they ridiculed only among themselves in private; they were old, the world had changed and they no longer had an active part in things which, in their youth, they had handled expertly, but very differently.

It was these old men who listened to the growing denunciations of Father Cross and his troublesome long-horn bulls, with silent, even sardonic humour. In their day a *vaquero* rode out to gather wild cattle expecting fights, occasionally injuries, and lots of risks. Among themselves they found only one thing to compare with their earlier riding days and the present — they had used horses and so did the present-day rangemen. In their view, right there the comparison ended.

But oldtimers were always a minority. One of them was the half-Mex, half *gringo* owner of the saloon in Coyanosa, a man as dark as old leather with startlingly light eyes, Jawn Kelly, whose father, of a less tolerant generation, had deliberately written on the birth certificate that his newborn son was named J-a-w-n, because if he had spelled it J-o-h-n, in a predominantly Spanish-speaking Territory, it would have been pronounced Juan. What happened, of course was that Jawn Kelly among Spanish-speakers, became a name that rhymed with 'Yawn'. Well, the old man had tried.

Jawn had grown up working long-horns, he was close to seventy, looked and acted fifty. He was liked throughout the countryside despite a forthright manner which ordinarily went with his variety of tolerant, good-natured personality.

He was a man of medium height, with the upper body of a wrestler, and spindly legs.

He dispensed liquor and very rarely drank it. Jawn Kelly was a widower without issue. He was very fond of children, loved good horseflesh, possessed a broad, warm smile and had one reserved table for oldtimers in a far corner of his business establishment near a front window where his elderly patrons could be warmed by winter suns and also watch the roadway while they nursed their five-cent glasses of beer and played match-stick poker.

Cyanosa's town marshal was a large, not overly tall Texan named Ellery — pronounced El Rey, or Elrey — Austin, whose neck and head were the same size, whose hands were the size of small hams, and whose general appearance was of a fair-headed, blue-eyed gorilla. Elrey maintained law and order, something that frequently put his capabilities to the test. Maybe the modern rangemen were no match for their wild predecessors, but their temperaments were about the same; after working hard for days on end, when they loped into Coyanosa, they were full of piss and vinegar.

Newcomers among them, usually seasonal hirelings, not infrequently ran afoul of Constable Austin. Oldtimers among them never did. As Jawn Kelly had remarked more than once, in every town at some time, every uninhibited buckaroo had to meet an Elrey Austin. In Coyanosa it happened almost every riding season.

Elrey was a reasonable individual, up to a point. Sometimes he exceeded his limit, but he had to be convinced forbearance and patience were warranted, otherwise he exercised his particular form of persuasion, at which he was very good.

Elrey was greying at the temples. It was slyly said he even wore his ivory-stocked sixgun to bed. With more candour and a smidgin of awe, it was also said that border-jumpers up out of *Mejico* or gringo renegades, rawhiders, fugitives, trouble-makers of any stripe, either did not linger in Coyanosa or remained there indefinitely, their choice.

Elrey was in his forties, at his prime. He was like iron when he had to be, otherwise he liked people and they liked him.

He and Jawn Kelly had been close friends for years. It perhaps was a good test of Elrey Austin's character that he was an unlucky gambler while Jawn Kelly was just the opposite; they had played poker almost every week for three or four years with Jawn almost always the winner.

And they remained close friends.

In early spring when the Middle Domain of New Mexico Territory was blessed with occasional warm rains, tall livestock feed, pleasant days and cool nights, it was the customary calving time for range stockmen, although with bulls running with cows year round, calves could come any time, but instinct or Mother Nature, or something anyway, ordained that most calves were born during a season when cows could make plenty of milk.

Seasons were unalterable, give or take a little. Mammy cows calved regularly, and the fourth year after Father Ambrosia of the Cross inaugurated his longhorn project, two things simultaneously occurred. One, of no immediate concern up in Coyanosa, there was an uprising down over the line in Old Mexico, and even that, like yucca plants, flourished and flowered with uneven but persistent regularity.

The other occurrence was a convocation of furious and determined cattlemen in Coyanosa with their spokesman a grizzled, quince-faced, weathered and lined prune of a man named Dodge Plummer, whose perpetually squinted blue eyes were unwavering in their regard of Constable Elrey Austin. There were four cattlemen in size and substance besides Dodge. Among the group they had at least thirty hired riders, a small army in the Coyanosa country.

Elrey knew about the priest's bulls. Having matured in cow camps he knew exactly what Father Cross's entrance into the livestock business was going to cause among ranchers who had shot longhorn bulls out of hand for twenty years, until they had become as scarce as hen's teeth; until the advent of the priest's longhorns.

Wild longhorn bulls were as wary as wolves, much faster, but not fast enough to out-run bullets. Until the priest's bulls roamed, there hadn't been a wild longhorn sighted in years, and that fact, coupled with the fresh invasion known to have begun with the holy father's undertaking, created an ambiguous situation.

As Dodge Plummer told Elrey Austin, four longhorn bulls had been shot miles from Coyanosa, and except that those dead ones had the Trinity band — a small cross on each side of a larger cross — the ancient mark of San Angelo Mission in its heyday when mission fathers had great herds of cattle, the stockman had wondered if those bulls hadn't been remnants of the wild bands they thought had been eliminated.

Now, Dodge Plummer told the constable, it was the intention of the cowmen for miles around, to shoot longhorn bulls on sight, and, Plummer growled, why didn't that confounded priest castrate bull calves like everyone else did?

Dodge Plummer was an oldtimer in

the Coyanosa country; he knew as well as anyone and better than most why longhorn bulls were not castrated. It was very simple; a longhorn steer grew almost as tall as a saddlehorse, but at least he put on weight and years ago he could be sold as beef. Longhorn bulls grew tall, their ribs usually showed even at the height of the seasons of plentiful feed, they were never fat simply because in their tiny minds their entire purpose for being alive was to roam over many miles seeking breedable cows. They had been known to walk forty miles in one day. That kind of critter was never fat.

Elrey invited the cowman up to Jawn Kelly's cantina where he stood the first round, and where Jawn Kelly listened to the angry talk as impassive as a stone.

Plummer said the cattlemen had met some time earlier. Their decision was to launch a longhorn-bull hunt, kill every one they saw, but even old Dodge Plummer was neither a vindictive nor entirely inconsiderate individual. What he and his companions had decided, was to meet in Coyanosa with their ultimatum. Either the priest sold all his damned razorback bulls and got rid of his mammy razorback cows, or the stockmen were going to take time out from their normal chores and begin a systematic hunt for the Trinity bulls and wipe them out.

Elrey weathered the storm of angry stockmen. He asked if any of them had talked to the priest. Dodge Plummer said no, they hadn't. It was the job of the local lawman to do that.

Elrey promised he would talk to Father Cross, everyone had another round and the cattlemen departed. The last word, spoken from the saloon doorway by a large, black-eyed, black-headed man with a wound for a mouth whose name was Jeffrey Mesa, was that Father Cross and the constable had one week, after that there would be no more meetings and the killing would begin.

After Jeff Mesa disappeared beyond the doors of the cantina, Jawn Kelly's pale gaze lingered in that direction as he said, 'Well, you knew it was going to happen sooner or later, so did I an' most other folks. But Jeff Mesa is a first class son of a bitch, and most folks know that too.'

Elrey leaned on the bartop considering the painting over the backbar of an English thoroughbred, whose neck was too long and scrawny for local taste but whose back, shoulders, forearms and rump were admirable; they were bred for speed.

Jawn rattled the constable's empty glass. Elrey brought his gaze down shaking his head. He smiled at the dark man with startlingly blue eyes. 'Cross is a good man. He wants above all else to see the old church repaired and maintained, and you can't blame him for that.'

Jawn was a practical individual. He was also a good Catholic. Those two things were not compatible with the present situation. 'What can you tell him?' he asked.

Elrey Austin raised his gaze to the English race horse again as he replied. 'Either castrate bull calves or the cattlemen will do what Jeff Mesa said.'

It was early spring when the semi-desert country of the Middle Domain was fragrant, pleasantly warm, and carpeted with good, strong grass, green browse, and flowing sump springs.

Elrey Austin went down through Mex town, past its large, dusty plaza with the old dug-well in the centre, and walked north to the outskirts where the mission stood.

It was old, had mud walls three feet thick, sunken little window slits, some with the original scraped-thin rawhide panes, was cool at the hottest time of year and warm during the chilly winters.

It had cells for brothers, none of whom still lived, a long rear gallery paved with hand-made red tiles, and below in the huge old dark cellar, was a wine room where in times past women and girls had walked barefoot to force

16

grapes to yield their juice to be made into wine.

No wine had been made in Mission San Angelo in fifty years. The congregation, mostly natives of Mexican descent, still trooped up there every Sunday, but in total numbers as well as in economic conditions, their offerings were pitifully inadequate, which was what had troubled the priest, whose born name had been Henry Moriarty but who had almost forgotten that name. He was in his sixties, had been a devout forty years and had been known as *Padre de la Cruz* — Father Of The Cross — for all of those years.

His delapidated final assignment had hurt his heart from his first sight of it. Neglect even extended to the burial area out back where stones and wooden headboards either leaned perilously or had already fallen to be overgrown.

He had worked like a mule, in fact that had become his fond name among the parishioners. The Little Mule. He had cleaned out the debris of a century of neglect, he had scrubbed and painted, swept and re-built, had performed Last Rites and baptisms, heard confessions and gave Rosary lessons among people whose fathers had seen the last priest at San Angelo Mission.

He was a ginger-haired, muscular, tireless small man, admired by even those who only knew of him through his dedication. He was loved by his parishioners.

He was held in esteem by Constable Austin who spent the afternoon after the meeting of angry cowmen, looking for him. Jawn Kelly had been baptised in the old Mission, both his *mestizo* mother and his Irish father had been devout. Jawn served at the altar when he could, like everyone else who knew the little priest. Jawn Kelly called himself a 'back-slider', which meant he did not attend services as often as he should have, but in the saloon business Saturday nights were long. Jawn slept away a good part of Sunday mornings.

2

A Long Day

Where they finally met was at the jacal of an old man whose illness, Father Cross told Elrey Austin, was probably terminal.

The old peon's numerous family was at bedside in a small, crowded room, so the priest took Elrey out back where they could talk.

The priest listened solemnly to what Constable Austin had to say. He did not interrupt and when Elrey was finished, Father Cross slowly nodded his head. He said he had heard rumours, and smiled. In Mex town people heard things and whispered them along; they seemed to hear things long before anyone did in the gringo part of Coyanosa; the reason, so it was said, was because after ten generations the natives were so close to the sky and the soil they picked up reverberations from those elements. Maybe, but for a fact whatever the reason, Mex town was a very good source of information.

Elrey leaned in the shade behind the dying man's jacal gazing in the direction of the massive old mission. Father Cross spread his hands, palms downward. 'I had an idea,' he said softly. 'The offerings are never enough, Elrey, and what has to be done cannot be done entirely by labour itself. For example, while the parishioners have made adobe bricks and have patched roof tiles, they cannot make steel hinges or repair damage only skilled artisans can do. But there was no money to pay these skilled people, so I had to figure out a way to get the money to pay for these other things. You understand?'

Elrey nodded. Of course he understood, had in fact understood before the priest spoke. 'Father,' he said quietly. 'Wasn't there some other way? You're not a cattleman.'

'No, I am not, but what other way was there to start something which would bring the money? In this country the main source of revenue is livestock, so . . .'

'Father, why didn't you talk to me first? You jumped in with your long-horns smack-dab into the centre of something you knew nothing about, which was simply that for a generation cattlemen in the Coyanosa country have been trying to get rid of longhorns. And Father — who told you to keep all your bull calves as bulls? No one has done that in a very long . . .'

'Elrey, bull calves gain faster, grow heavier.' The priest made his hand gesture again. 'I scraped together every cent I could find to buy the first cows and bulls. Longhorns were the cheapest and they thrive where purebred cattle starve. You see?'

'Father, I understand all this, but I just told you what has happened. Hereford cows bought and up-graded at considerable expense to meet current

21

beef requirements, are now threatened by your longhorn bulls. You have to appreciate the position of men like Dodge Plummer and Feliciano Cortez and Jeff Mesa; your razorbacks are threatening their livelihoods. You can't just buy scrub cattle and turn them loose among purebreds. Father, men have been killed for less than what you've done.'

'Elrey, it is open country. It is free range.'

Constable Austin was losing patience. 'Listen to me, Father: they are going to make a shooting war against your cattle. They're going to send their riders out with rifles to kill every critter with the trinity band they can find.'

The priest looked around at the constable. 'You are the law,' he said, and Elrey felt like swearing, instead he sighed loudly and said, 'I know it's open range. I know every argument you're goin' to use.'

'If they shoot my cattle as the law it will be your duty . . . '

'Father, the range is maybe a thousand miles. The only way I'll know about your dead cattle will be if I see buzzards circling. I can't arrest buzzards. What's more, I want to stop this before it gets to that point.'

'What do you want me to do, Elrey? How else can I raise the money for the mission?'

'Father, I don't know how else you can raise money. I don't know anything about something like that, but I *do* know if you don't get rid of those damned bulls we're goin' to have trouble up to our gullets. I can tell you something else you don't know but I do know; if this kind of a war starts it won't be just the stockmen against you and your cattle; people will take sides. You understand what I'm saying?'

'Yes.'

'Then please . . . help me to keep all this from happening.'

'How?'

'I told you, Father; get rid of those damned longhorns.'

The little priest sat on a wooden bucket, hands clasped between his knees, the epitome of dejection. He was quiet so long the constable felt uncomfortable. A young child with large black eyes came to speak in soft Spanish.

Father Cross nodded and arose. Before entering the jacal he said, 'He has died,' and left Elrey standing in shade.

On his way back to his *juzgado* office Constable Austin nodded to people he knew in Mex town. One was a grizzled, dark man on horseback whose raw-hide reins and monkey-face tapaderas showed considerable use. His name was Ramon Baca, but throughout the Coyanosa country where he had been a working rangeman for forty years, he was known simply as Chief, the Anglo version of *jefe*. He was one of the oldtimers whose tireless body and healthy outlook kept him in the saddle after most men his age got down and never climbed up again.

Chief Baca was one of less than a handful who had worked longhorns in the old days. He had been a tophand then and was still a tophand, which was probably where he had acquired his nickname.

He was tallish, lean, lined and grey-headed. As he drew rein and greeted the constable, his shrewd dark eyes with their muddy whites were stone-steady. He leaned on the saddle-horn. 'They are mad as hell,' he said.

Elrey, who needed no elaboration, nodded his head. 'I know. I met Dodge, Jeff and the others a while back.'

' . . . Well?'

'I don't know, Chief, but I told Father Cross he is going to be responsible for a damned war if he don't do something about those bulls.'

Baca sighed, still softly smiling. 'You know why he started with longhorns, don't you?'

'Hell yes I know, and I sympathise, but what he's done wouldn't even have been right when you were young. At

25

least in those days they castrated their bull calves . . . Chief, if he sells them, gets rid of them, he'll get a little money. If he don't round them up, corral them somewhere and sell them . . . they'll end up shot an' he won't get anything for them.'

Baca continued to lean on his saddlehorn and smile downward. 'There is a revolution down over the line,' he said, changing a subject which he probably had concluded could only end with lots of repetition and no solution.

Elrey squinted up at the older man. 'Nothing new about that. As long as it don't spill over the border . . . ' Elrey shrugged.

Chief Baca had another bit of information, this time capturing the constable's full attention. 'You heard about that band of renegades out of Texas who raided some villages last winter? Well, last week they raided a gringo encampment on the north fork of Alamos River.'

Alamos River was northeast of Coyanose about a hundred miles. There was a settlement over there called Harpersville.

'Bad?' Elrey asked.

Baca inclined his head a little. 'Massacred the wagon people, carried off the women, killed the animals and fired the wagons.'

'You're sure?'

'Yes. Boss Cleaver of Plummer's crew came back from Harpersville a couple of days ago. He saw what was left of the encampment.'

'Where was the army?' Elrey asked, and listened with understanding to Chief Baca's bitter laugh. 'The army, companero, was where it always is, chasing a trail of Indians.' Baca's smile remained, cold now and bitter. 'Many miles northward.' Baca paused. 'What Indians? There have been no hostile Indians in the Harpersville country for six or eight years. Not every band of barefoot horses has men on their backs, eh?'

27

Elrey glanced elsewhere. Two small boys were having difficulties herding a mixed band of sheep and goats toward their home corral.

A handsome woman with pigeon-wings of grey at both temples watched for a while then called to the boys to concentrate on one or two ewes and nannies. It worked, the other animals followed the females.

Chief looked over at the woman and called something in Spanish. She leaned in shade of a ramada considering Elrey and the vaquero for a moment, then turned back to enter her home with a shrug and called back, this time in English.

'I have goat *fajitas* and no wine. Suit yourself.'

Chief Baca moved his rein hand, winked at Elrey and rode in the direction of the woman's residence.

Elrey continued through the late day, stopped at the cafe for supper then went over to his empty jailhouse where it was cool, and dark until he lighted the hanging lamp.

Someone had once told him trouble comes in threes. The revolution southward over the line in Mexico, those murderous, drunken, pitiless raiders were back after a quiet winter, and those damned longhorn bulls!

The following afternoon he was at Jawn Kelly's saloon when a red-faced, bulky man with thinning light brown hair appeared in town, tied up out front and shouldered into the saloon.

Elrey nodded to him and Jawn set up a bottle and glass as he said, 'You been away?'

The red-faced man nodded and poured without spilling, raised the little glass with a steady hand to drop the whiskey straight down. He gasped, rolled his eyes and blew out a flammable breath before speaking.

'Went over to Harpersville for kegs of horseshoes for Dodge.'

Jawn's brows dropped a notch. 'Is Dodge short-handed; why send his

29

range boss on a job a chore-boy could do?'

The bulky man was re-filling his jolt glass when he answered. 'Because there was some ranch freight to also be picked up.' Boss Cleaver downed his second drink and went through the same grimacing routine, which was ignored by Jawn Kelly and the constable.

Elrey said, 'Trouble over there, Boss?'

Cleaver turned, sweat making his face shiny. 'Gawddamn big band of renegades wiped out a wagon camp.' The red-faced man scowled. 'Murdering sons of bitches. Folks at Harpersville was scairt peeless. Where they wiped out them emigrants wasn't no more than ten, twelve miles from town!' Cleaver turned back toward Jawn Kelly. 'Big band of 'em. The fellers from town who rode out at sight of smoke rising, come back to Harpersville with a guess that there was maybe twenty of them Comancheros or whatever they are. Lawless, murdering, drunken, stealin', damned renegade scum.' Cleaver eyed the bottle, scowled and twisted to face Elrey Austin. 'Whites, 'breeds, Messicans, leave nothin' after they attack. Dead womenfolk, men, little kids, horses an' mules.'

Boss struck the countertop with a big fist. 'They sent riders from Harpersville for the army. Hell of a lot of good that done; word come back the army's ridin' itself ragged on the trail of barefoot horses someone says was rode by In'ians. You know what I think? I think the government ought to recall all its soldiers an' let us go back to the way things was done when I was a kid — round up every able-bodied man with guns an' run 'em down if it took a month, and left 'em hanging or shot where they was found.'

For a moment there was not a sound. The saloon was empty and would remain so for another hour or two. Elrey asked what direction the renegades took after leaving the scene of the massacre.

Dodge Plummer's rangeboss shook his head. 'North. Straight north.'

That was encouraging. If they went far enough north they would be in the territory around a town called Guadalupe; it was as large as Harpersville and Coyanosa combined. It also had a military post west of town about two miles.

Boss shook his head over the obvious thoughts of his companions. 'They'll veer off. Only thing you got to give men like that credit for, is being *coyote*. They can smell soldiers. They can sniff up big vigilante crowds too . . . Well, this ain't gettin' the supplies an' mail I come to town for.'

Dodge Plummer's beefy rangeboss dug out several silver coins, dropped them atop the bar, nodded and walked out into bright daylight.

Elrey finished nursing his warm beer and said nothing as Jawn went to re-fill the glass. When Jawn returned he said, 'He's right. Even if the army arrives it's always days late. Vigilantes are the answer, Elrey.'

Constable Austin half-heartedly agreed. He had never been enthusiastic about citizen posses. He had seen their excesses. On the other hand when renegade bands struck they were usually well mounted, armed to the teeth, and arrived like a cyclone so that even if town constables were ready, they could do little without help.

Jawn turned philosophical. Coyanosa had met its share of Indian raiders, Mexican border-jumpers, horsethieves and a few hold-up men, but it had never been hit by one of those large, lawless bands of marauders who wanted more than a village could offer.

Elrey went down to the cafe for supper, locked the jailhouse up for the night and went over to the adobe hotel, once a barracks for detachments of Mexican soldiers when the southwest had belonged to Old Mexico, and sat out front on the cool, shaded old veranda to ponder again his immediate problem, Father Cross's damned long-horn bulls.

It was a cool evening, fragrant as a result of spring's wild flowers curing on the stem, peaceful in all directions.

He sighed, arose and went to his room to bed down. The world — his world anyway — seemed to deliberately lull people. Nature, or something anyway, had a treacherous heart. War down over the line, bands of pitiless marauders riding over the land again — and those damned longhorn bulls!

Elrey went to sleep thinking of old Dodge Plummer, the way he had looked and spoken when last they had met. The southward revolution, even the wild-riding murderers were forgotten. He had to do something about Father Cross's longhorns; not just think about it, but *do* something, not next week or next month, he had to do something about it tomorrow!

3

Something Different

Longhorns were extraordinary cattle by any comparison. Despite the grisly promises of Dodge Plummer and other stockmen, shooting the priest's wild cattle would require more than excellent marksmanship. Longhorns, even those raised close, had a wild streak. They were more wary and spooky than any other large four-legged critter.

No solitary hunter or group of longhorn-hunting rangemen would get within gunrange before they were seen, and the cattle fled.

Chasing them on horseback wore down good horses, ruined the dispositions of rangemen, and rarely resulted in dead longhorns.

There were a few, like Chief Baca, who had come to manhood working wild cattle, otherwise later generations of riders were not *coyote* enough, nor tough enough, to get close enough to use guns, nor corral them in a box canyon somewhere.

It was the wiliness of longhorns as much as their courting purebred cows, that had rangemen raging until the air turned blue. It was, as an oldtimer or two had noted, being made fools of more than anything else that had the Dodge Plummers of the countryside steaming mad. No one, particularly rangemen whose trappings were symbolic of a hallowed, traditional brotherhood, wanted to be made a fool of, especially by something as slab-sided, wicked-horned long legged, temperamentally unpredictable as Father Cross's damned mongrel bulls.

Elrey Austin had an early breakfast before going down to the old mission, where he found Father Cross, robe hitched above knees, wielding a heavy hoe in a large vegetable patch where other people were also working because if this was done early enough, by the time heat arrived everyone could be safely back in cool adobe houses.

Father Cross loosened his girdling rope, let the robe fall, leaned his hoe aside and joined the constable on the long old cool veranda that ran the full length of the mission.

They sat. The priest mopped sweat off with a limp bandana and watched his parishioners working as he said, 'I thought last night. I prayed . . . '

'And?' Elrey asked quietly.

The priest sighed, still watching the workers out in the morning sunlight. 'How do I get them?'

'Get them?'

'My cattle. They are only the Lord knows where. I'm no rider. Even if I was, where would I put them if I caught them?'

Constable Austin also watched the workers in the vegetable garden. 'Does this mean you'll quit raising them?'

'Yes. But how do I corral them, and

where?' Father Cross made his fluttery little hand gesture. 'I could sell them if they were corralled where a buyer could see them. I would get a little money; if they are shot . . . ' A shrug.

Elrey leaned to give the smaller man a light pat on the shoulders. He was relieved. He had been sure that when they met this morning the holy father was going to argue. 'There is a way, Father,' Elrey said, arising from the bench.

'How?' the small man asked looking up: 'I don't even know where they are.'

Elrey looked down. 'Finding them will take time but it can be done. Corralling them . . . I don't know. They're wild and pretty *coyote*.'

He left the priest sitting there. He had arrived at the mission with little hope. On his way back to the jailhouse office, while the next problem was in his mind, he was relieved that at least the priest had been willing to get rid of his longhorns.

He went up to Jawn Kelly's cantina.

Jawn and Chief Baca were rattling in Spanish, switched to English when Elrey walked in, and let him get comfortable against the bar before Jawn said, '*Pronunciados* crossed the border last night.'

Elrey looked from Kelly to Chief Baca. 'How do you know?'

The dark man smiled. '*Arrieros* coming north with their laden pack mules saw them, sneaked down and spied on their camp.'

'Where?'

Baca shrugged. 'Ten, maybe fifteen miles south.'

'How many?'

'Maybe fifteen. Maybe twenty.'

Elrey nodded and Jawn brought three beers. He ordinarily did not drink with customers, but ragged, fierce raiders from below the border near Coyanosa was cause for serious worry.

They were as wild and ruthless as the other terror of the southwest; mixed gangs of fierce and murderous renegades, the kind Boss Cleaver had seen sign of over at Harpersville.

Baca half emptied his glass before speaking again. 'Their uprising must be in trouble. The only safety they have if a Mex army is chasing them, is to cross over into our country where the soldiers will not follow.'

Jawn drily said, 'I'd never bet money on that, either.'

Elrey ignored the remark. Right now he did not even think of longhorn cattle. A band of border-jumpers in his area could mean more trouble than a man could shake a stick at.

He asked if Chief Baca had told Dodge Plummer, and got a brisk nod of the head along with the answer. 'This morning. The *arrieros* passed the yard. We fed them, listened and sent them on their way. Dodge sent men in all directions to gather riders.'

'To do what?' Elrey asked.

'Be ready if they come north. Ready and waiting.' Baca smiled. 'Dodge has been through this before. Many times. Before I rode to town for ammunition this morning he was acting like a young man; he likes something like this. He even joked with us.'

Neither Kelly nor the constable smiled. Baca was a free spirit. He looked forward to the change from doing routine cattle work. His last word to Elrey before heading down to the general store for boxes of ammunition, was: 'Send scouts south. Get ready. *Adios compañeros.*'

Elrey went to the blacksmith shop where his information was greeted with silence. He asked the blacksmith to scout southward, which the smith agreed to do and closed his shop leaving his leather apron lying across an anvil.

Words spread fast. Merchants brought their wares inside off the plankwalks, shuttered their glass windows with bullet proof slabs of heavy steel which had not been closed in years.

People milled like sheep agitatedly discussing the possibility of a raid.

Elmer Beedle the gunsmith whose shop was north of the cantina and who had not done much business in months, was suddenly overwhelmed by gunbuyers along with others who owned weapons needing repair.

To avoid being stopped and questioned, Elrey told Jawn to send armed men to the jailhouse where he intended to organise a defence force, which he had never been required to do before since becoming the local lawman, but which posed no particular problem because it had been done before by other constables in this kind of an emergency, and men converged on the jailhouse until it was full.

Elrey's plan was simple; nothing would be done beyond preparing, until the blacksmith returned with news of the whereabouts of the invaders. If he returned to say the border jumpers were heading for Coyanosa, Elrey would have someone ring the bell at the fire house and whatever was required would then be done.

Whether this satisfied the agitated townsmen he had no idea, but since he appeared to be the person to whom emergency authority was delegated, he was not going to be stampeded. Not until he knew the raiders were coming.

Acting on a hunch he went down to Mex town. If anyone had information on border jumpers it would be down there.

At the cantina on the west side of the plaza he encountered stony silence. The patrons were armed to the teeth. They watched Elrey reach the counter and place his back to it to ask what was known.

One man, older than most in the room, said his brother had heard of border jumpers yesterday afternoon. They had been heading north. Beyond that all he knew was that it was a large band, and as the result of a pitched battle south of the border in which the rebels had been defeated with great loss, this particular band had fled for the border and got across it with

Rurales and Mexican regulars shooting at them.

Elrey asked about the constabulary troops and regulars. The old man shook his head. They had stopped at the border, but, he said, the custom was to bivouac down there and wait for the *pronunciados* to return. If that happened there would be no quarter.

The day wore along. When the blacksmith eventually returned it was late afternoon. He was dusty, sweaty and astride an exhausted horse.

Elrey heard the shouting as the blacksmith loped into town and was out front of the jailhouse as the blacksmith stepped to the ground, looped his reins, brushed past Elrey to go directly to the hanging olla and thirstily drink before sinking down upon a wall bench with fresh perspiration running, and said, 'Well, they was down there. I guess it was too far for folks to hear the shooting.'

The blacksmith raised a sleeve to mop sweat off before continuing. 'It was maybe forty or fifty of 'em — *bandoleros* of the worst kind. They'd stole horses somewhere this side of the border because they was well mounted.

'The feller leadin' them was a rawboned red-headed feller in a dirty uniform. He looked more like a Texan than a Mexican. But he was Mex; I heard them yelling his name. Salcedo.'

Elrey said, 'How close?'

The blacksmith went to the olla again before answering. 'They ain't coming,' he said, dropping back down on the bench.

Elrey stared.

'They was breakin' camp when I come up atop a little hill. They was out in flat country so they couldn't see as well as I could. They was takin' their time. I looked southeasterly and hell, there was a column of cavalry comin' in a slow lope with videttes and scouts out front.

'When they was close enough someone blew a bugle.' The blacksmith paused to smile in recollection. 'They

45

didn't see the US cavalry because of my little hill, but they heard that bugle. It was like kickin' an ant hill. They yelled and ran for their horses, left blankets and whatnot where they was. That red-headed feller had a sword. He waved it in the air and yelled his head off as he turned south back toward the border.

'What happened was that because them 'Merican cavalry was comin' from the southeast, they was below the Messicans ... Damndest thing; them Mexicans ran like scairt rabbits with the red-headed feller out front ... They didn't seem to know how close the bluebellies was until that feller with the bugle blew another blast and the bluebellies charged into them *bandoleros* from southward.

'For a few minutes it was a hell of a jumble of confusion and shouting and gunshots. The bluebellies chased them marauders straight toward Mexico. I don't know whether they caught the rest of them or not, but there was a mess of them lyin' back where they'd been shot. And loose horses running everywhere.

'I came back.'

Elrey went slowly to his desk, dug out his bottle of whiskey and handed it to the blacksmith, who regarded it for a long time then handed it back. 'Not as empty as my belly is,' he said, and arose, went to the door, smiled tiredly and went out into the cooling early evening.

Elrey waited until supper time before leaving the jailhouse. He wanted the blacksmith's story to have spread before he headed for the cafe.

By nightfall the townspeople knew their dread had been resolved. Some, who ordinarily did not have a good word for the army, were liberal with their praise.

At Kelly's saloon toasts were proposed for everyone beginning with the President in Washington, down to the lowliest dog-robber among the soldiers.

When Elrey finally bedded down he

fell asleep without once thinking about the problem which had engrossed him until news of armed border-jumpers had arrived in Coyanosa, but he awakened in the morning thinking of it, and went down to the cafe thinking about it.

Jawn Kelly was at the cafe counter. He nodded to Elrey as the constable sank down beside him. Kelly said, 'You sleep good last night?'

'Yes. Did you?'

Instead of replying Jawn showed a sour expression and reached for his coffee cup.

Later, with the unexpected arrival in town of Dodge Plummer accompanied by what looked like a small army of armed men, Elrey held the door for the cowman to enter his jailhouse office and expected a tirade. Instead the older man sat down and wagged his head. 'Damned army spoilt the fun. We was organised to go hunt them border jumpers down and pitch into them.'

Elrey sat at his desk considering the

vinegary old rancher. Plummer sighed, shoved out saddle-warped legs and considered the toes of his scuffed boots as he spoke again.

'One trouble resolved, which leaves us with the one we had before. You talked to the priest?'

'He's agreeable to getting rid of his cattle.'

Dodge looked surprised. 'Well ... that'll maybe take care of things, won't it?'

Elrey was candid. 'Depends on how many of his bulls can be found, an' how they are to be corralled.'

Plummer was old enough to have worked wild cattle. 'Takes a bit of doing,' he replied. 'It'd be simpler to shoot 'em, Constable. They're sons of bitches to handle an' right this minute I can't imagine how Father Cross figures to do it. But I'll tell you this: We aren't goin' to wait forever; if he don't figure something out quick ... '

Plummer arose, re-set his shapeless old hat, nodded and walked out into the roadway leaving Elrey sitting thoughtfully at his desk.

Elrey could not imagine, either, how those longhorns were to be caught. As for Father Cross, he had never pretended to be a stockman. The responsibility would be his, but no one including Constable Austin, would delude themselves into believing the little priest would know how to capture his trinity cattle.

Elrey was over in front of the general store after having supper when that handsome woman with the pigeon-wing streaks of grey over her temples came out of the store and stopped.

They exchanged greetings. The woman's name was Carmen Bohorquez. She knew about the soldiers catching the border jumpers. She also knew something else; Ramon Baca was to ride in from the Plummer ranch tonight for a dinner she was preparing for the two of them.

Elrey softly rubbed his nose about that. The handsome woman was a widow; he had no idea of the marital status of Chief Baca nor did he dwell upon it. He had enough to occupy his thoughts without minding the personal affairs of others.

He told her he was sure Baca would enjoy her supper. She smiled and walked away. He watched until she turned down a sideroad, then went up to the saloon.

4

Raw Nerves

Jawn Kelly responded in his practical manner when Elrey complained about the predicament of the longhorn bulls and the priest. He said, 'I get old men in here every day or two who worked them longhorns.'

Elrey did not look mollified. 'They haven't been on horses in ten years. Besides that, even if they was willing, that kind of work would likely kill them off.'

Jawn was polishing glasses and did not look up when he said, 'They ain't all helpless, Elrey. Talk to Chief Baca. He done it when he was young and he's still one of the best stockmen in the country.'

Elrey gazed at the dark man with the startlingly blue eyes for a long time, then slapped the countertop and marched out of the saloon.

Night had arrived, there were lights in all directions. He walked without haste down to the Mex town plaza, which was empty, but there were also lights down there, not as bright because Mex town's inhabitants used candles, which were easy to make and cost considerably less than coal oil.

He approached the *chozo* of the widow Borhorquez and stopped at sight of a dozing horse tied out front. Chief had arrived, was probably having supper with the handsome woman; he would welcome being interrupted by Constable Austin about as much as having a scorpion in his boot.

Elrey sauntered close, found a faggot corral which smelled powerfully of goats, and leaned there. He needed a conversation with Baca and did not want to put it off or make the long ride out to the Plummer ranch tomorrow or the next day.

He sighed, hitched at his shellbelt

and walked to the front of the lighted small house. For a moment he hesitated before knocking on the door. Inside, a light happy conversation abruptly stopped.

Carmen Bohorquez opened the door. Even by weak candle light her face looked flushed from cooking. She eyed Elrey and sighed, turned without a word and told her guest who was outside.

She never did say a word to the constable. After Chief walked out she closed the door behind him. He considered Elrey as he might have considered a tarantula.

Elrey apologised, then launched into an explanation for his visit. Baca, darker than ever in ramada shade, deliberately rolled and lighted a cigarette before speaking. He did not ask how Elrey had known he would be at the widow's house, but he did say, 'I thought only cats could see in the dark.'

Elrey waited.

'Well, first there must be a big corral.

The priest can find men who know how to build a high, very strong one. Remember, those cattle of his can jump almost as high as a horse. Sometimes even higher. And the corral must be made very strong because when long-horns are upset or frightened, they close their eyes and go through fences.'

Elrey accepted these words of wisdom with no misgivings. He said, 'Where?'

'The corral?' Chief Baca shrugged. 'Anywhere, but if he means to get cattle buyers here, maybe it should be on the outskirts of town. Maybe at the north end because that's the route the bulls will travel to reach it.'

Elrey's brows dropped a notch. 'They won't come within a mile of Coyanosa, Chief.'

The dark man exhaled smoke. 'I tell you what, *jefe*. Get the corral built a hundred or so yards north of town and make sure it could withstand elephants. Since the Holy Father needs help, leave it up to me to get his damned bulls to the corral.'

Elrey waited until the dark man had stamped out his smoke. He wanted to ask questions but Chief Baca turned toward the closed door as he said, 'If you start the corral tomorrow, make it big. Most of all make it strong, very, very strong.' He was reaching for the drawstring when he said, 'I'll come to town day after tomorrow to see how good the corral will be. That has to come first; there would be no point in driving the bulls down here to the corral if they could smash it. Good night, Elrey.'

Constable Austin's dismissal had been final. He started back toward his part of town. When he got out front of Kelly's saloon there were horses at the rack and loud noises from inside.

He went to the hotel and bedded down, but sleep was a while arriving. The only thought he had to fall back on was Chief Baca's calm understanding and his pronouncements which had been made in the manner of a man who knew precisely what he was talking about.

On the other hand, Elrey had never worked wild cattle but he had heard many tales from those who had, and not once had any of those stories mentioned corraling longhorns within scenting distance of a town. Not once.

In the morning after breakfast he was in the jailhouse when the bird-like older man who owned the general store arrived. He had an annoying habit of sniffing, was probably unaware when he did it, but others *were* aware.

He did not sniff until he had taken a chair and smiled feebly at the lawman across the little room. 'I heard them Messican border jumpers cut back, ducked around the soldiers and are heading back up this way. Elrey, I got an awful lot to lose if they attack Coyanosa.'

The constable sat with clasped hands eyeing his guest, who sniffed, folded and unfolded both hands in his lap.

'I can't say what you heard is wrong,

but with the US cavalry behind 'em, and one of those Mex route armies in front . . . ' Elrey shook his head without completing the remark.

'But you don't know,' the merchant exclaimed. 'All folks want is for someone to go down yonder an' make blessed sure them murderers are gone. That's all.'

The merchant sniffed.

Elrey leaned back off his desk. If the merchant's story was abroad, and Elrey would have bet money that it was, then just for the sake of appearance he would have to ride southward to be sure there were no border jumpers still in the area.

He told the merchant he would ride southward, after which the older man sniffed and departed, relieved if not exactly happy.

Elrey killed a half hour in the cool office before going out back and saddling one of two horses corralled back there.

He left town by a dusty alley, warmed

out his animal for better than a mile, then boosted him over into a rocking-chair lope.

There was considerable distance involved. It was not hot when Elrey left Coyanosa and would not get hot until he was a long way southward. But the ride back in the afternoon would be through Purgatory with sunlight in his face every blessed step of the way.

Two hours farther along he saw three grazing horses with saddles and bridles. They saw him and threw up their heads ready to run if he left the road in their direction.

Maybe on the return ride; right now he wanted to find the blacksmith's little hill and get up there before daylight departed.

He really was not interested in catching those horses except that, wearing sweaty saddle blankets under saddles and the direct sun, would scald their backs.

He made excellent time, found the little hill and climbed off atop it so his horse could rest while he studied the countryside.

He saw lumps which were dead men. He also saw buzzards already at work fighting among themselves and squawking. What he did not see, and he hunkered up there for more than an hour, was horsemen of any kind, army riders or Mexicans.

He rode back down off the little hill heading back, and sure enough, along with heat he had sunlight in his eyes.

The loose horses bearing huge-horned Mexican saddles were nowhere in sight. Elrey made no hunt for them. When he reached town he would pass word that the horses were down there. There was always someone who would go catch them.

When he got back it was late dusk. He cared for the horse then went over to the cafe, glancing in the direction of the general store as he hiked along. It was closed for the night. Probably because the nervous-nelly who owned it had received no word to the contrary about border jumpers, he had closed and locked the heavy steel shutters across his widows.

Most patrons of the cafe had eaten long ago. Elrey and the cafeman had the place almost to themselves. The cafeman liked to talk, but tonight Elrey was not in the mood; he had ridden his tail raw for nothing, had known that would be the extent of his sortie before leaving town.

Later, he went down to the mission where Father Cross was patching worn huarachas by candle light, straddling a saddlemaker's sewing horse. At his side on a bench was a glass of red wine.

When Elrey appeared through the darkness the priest abandoned his work, offered Elrey some wine, and climbed off the sewing horse, which he'd had to straddle, to go sit upon the same bench Elrey sank down upon.

Elrey told the priest what Chief Baca had said. The holy man's reaction was the same as Elrey's had been. 'A hundred or so yards north of town?

Elrey, I know almost nothing about cattle.'

Elrey nodded in darkness about that.

'But my bull, even the old cows, are very wild. Are you sure Ramon Baca said a hundred or so yards above town?'

'His exact words, Father.' He repeated himself about the strength of the corral. 'Big enough to hold many critters and so strong and high the worst bull you have can't bust out ... And he'll ride in day after tomorrow to look at what you've accomplished. Tell me, Father, can you find the men to build your corral? Will they have the tools?'

Father Cross nodded his head indifferently. ' . . . A hundred or so yards above town?'

Elrey nodded and sighed resignedly. 'Will you start work tomorrow?'

' . . . Yes, and suppose we build such a corral and the bulls cannot be driven into it?'

Elrey had doubted the idea when Chief Baca had suggested it, but since then he had yielded to the very persuasive idea that Chief Baca never would have made the suggestion unless he had thought it would work.

To the priest's worried question, Elrey simply said, 'I worked cattle years ago. Not longhorns. You never have but Chief Baca's worked all kinds of cattle. Father, unless you can come up with a better idea, start work on the corral tomorrow.'

The little priest shrugged. 'As you said, I don't know anything about these things. What other choice is there?'

'None. Believe in Chief. I'm as sceptical as you are, but I know if anyone knows longhorns it is Chief Baca . . . By the way, there are some loose saddle animals wearing Mex outfits south a half-day's ride, down where the US cavalry caught those border jumpers. I saw three but there are probably more. Pass the word among your friends; anyone who needs a horse and Mex outfit can go down there and catch one, or more than one.'

Elrey got to his feet. He was tired and having eaten heightened the feeling. He walked back to his jailhouse office, lighted the lamp and dropped into his chair behind the desk.

If he'd been feeling mean he could have gone over to the storekeeper's residence and routed him out of bed to tell him there were no damned *bandoleros* on their way to raid Coyanosa.

It was the storekeeper's fault he'd put in a miserable day.

By the time he bedded down Kelly's saloon was dark and quiet. It was never very alive on week-day nights.

Before sunrise the following morning Elrey went out back to the wash house and took an all-over bath before putting on clean clothes and hiking down to the cafe, where lights were burning and the roadway window was already fogged over even though there were as yet only two customers, Elrey Austin and Jawn Kelly. After bringing their platters the garrulous, slovenly cafeman said, 'There was a feller in here yestiddy, a travelin' peddler from up north . . . He told me there was talk up around Guadalupe of renegades raiding the outlying ranches.'

Elrey remembered what Boss Cleaver had said and downed half his coffee before commenting. 'They got a garrison of soldiers up there.'

The cafeman nodded about that and was distracted by the arrival of more customers. Jawn Kelly finished first, he had grown to manhood eating fast for several reasons; it was one of those habits formed early on that a man never shed, even long after there was no need for it.

'Their army'll take care of 'em,' Jawn said with confidence born of what had happened down south. 'When I went out back to pee this morning I seen half a dozen mounted Messicans with lass ropes leavin' town riding south.'

Elrey explained about the loose horses, finished his meal and went out front with the saloonman. They paused to breathe deeply of the fresh, cool

65

pre-daylight air, then Jawn hiked in the direction of his cantina and Elrey went down to the general store where the owner was working inside with his roadway door locked.

Elrey pounded until the sparrow-built nervous older man opened the door, then told him there were no border jumpers heading for town, did not wait to be thanked but walked over to unlock the jailhouse and make a pot of coffee.

Like Jawn Kelly and others around town when the rumour spread of renegades up north, Elrey Austin was disinclined to dwell on a band of renegades after what had happened to the border jumpers.

He was drinking black coffee when Jeff Mesa rode up, tied his horse out front and, because he wore Chihuahua spurs with their huge rowels, every step he took was noisy.

He entered the jailhouse, wrinkled his nose at the aroma of coffee, and after being told to help himself, the dark-eyed rancher did not even offer a greeting until he was seated with hot java in one gloved hand. Then he said, 'Had to come to town anyway, so figured I'd see what you'n the priest worked out about his damned bulls.'

Elrey did not like Jeffrey Mesa, few people did, he was brusque and overbearing. He was also a successful cowman with a large holding, three permanent riders and hundreds of cattle.

'He's goin' to sell them,' Elrey stated.

Jeff Mesa snorted. 'Not without rounding them up for a buyer to look at.' Mesa drained the cup and also said, 'He'll be lucky to get five dollars a head. Those cattle are more trouble than they're worth.' He leaned to place the cup on the edge of Elrey's desk instead of going to the bucket of water beside the stove to sink it as everyone else did.

Elrey eyed the cup as he said, 'The idea is to get them off the range.'

Mesa agreed. 'Yes. The best way to

do that is to shoot 'em on sight. Day before yesterday I was coming up out of a draw near a spring. The damned bull was broadside to me drinking. He must have heard something because he threw up his head just as I fired . . . I had to drag the carcass down the draw.'

Elrey said nothing for a moment or two. Mesa was lunging up to his feet when the constable finally spoke. 'Dodge said the priest would be given time to get rid of them.'

Mesa looked down at the seated man. 'Dodge don't commit me or my riders to anything. What he wants to do is his business, as long as he does it on his range.' Mesa smiled bleakly. 'I got riders out with rifles and a bounty of a silver cartwheel for every trinity bull they kill.'

Elrey arose slowly as Mesa was turning toward the door. 'I wouldn't do that if I was you,' he said quietly, bringing Jeff Mesa around to stare a moment before speaking.

'I'll tell you the same thing I'd tell

Dodge. I'm the one who makes the rules on my land. Not Dodge, an' not you.'

Elrey started slowly around the desk. 'You shoot his bulls and it'll stir up the countryside. He's agreed to get rid of them. He needs a little time to do it . . . Don't shoot any more of them.'

Jeff Mesa's eyes widened. He recognised the signs even though Elrey had not raised his voice. 'I'm goin' to pay to have every one we see shot. It's not your business. It's been a couple weeks since we all met here in town and nothing's been done.'

'I'll make it my business,' Elrey said, walking slowly to close the distance between them.

'What'll you do?' Mesa asked with a sneer.

Elrey's strike was almost too fast to see, it doubled the other man over. Elrey stepped back, waited until the gasping lessened then said, 'You got a gun, Jeff.'

69

Mesa came up very slowly, he had been hurt. He stood sucking air for a long moment then snarled a bawling curse and sprang.

Elrey stepped aside. As the clawed hands swept past he stepped back and knocked Mesa to his knees with a blow to the back of his head.

Mesa would not go down; he hung there with his head down, body braced by both hands and his knees like a gutshot bear.

Elrey stepped to the water bucket, filled a dipper and threw it into Mesa's face. After that the dark-eyed man got sluggishly upright.

Elrey tapped his chest with a stiff finger. 'Give the priest a little time. Hell, it's past breeding time for most cows anyway. Do you hear me?'

Mesa's recovery was slow. He shuffled to the recently vacated chair, sank down and looked steadily at the man who had hurt him.

'Austin, goddamn you, I'll be back,' he muttered.

Elrey picked up Mesa's hat, jammed it on his head and jerked a thumb toward the door. 'Come back any time you want, Jeff. If I hear of you or any of your men shooting any more of those trinity cattle, you won't have to come lookin' for me, I'll come lookin' for you.'

Mesa had a sour taste in his mouth. He stood up, re-set his hat and went to the door. As he was opening it he made another threat.

'The ranchers'll like to know you're takin' the side of that damned priest. They'll want to hear about you threatening me.'

After Mesa's departure Elrey drank from the olla and sat on a wall bench.

That hadn't been the wisest thing he'd ever done. Mesa was a vindictive individual, by the time he spread his story among the ranchers, exactly what Elrey had wanted to avoid, serious trouble, would probably erupt.

He went toward the saloon and

stopped mid-way. There was an old wagon and half a dozen men north of town on the west side of the stage road, working in the heat at building a large corral.

5

Mucho Trabajo

The same day Elrey and Jeff Mesa had fought, but after dusk, old Dodge Plummer rode into town, tied up in front of the jailhouse and entered.

There was no one in the office. He lighted the hanging lamp, got comfortable in a chair beside the roadway door and waited.

Elrey was at the blacksmith's shop and saw the light. He had gone down there to arrange for the blacksmith to take one of his horses down to his shop in the morning and re-shoe him.

On the way to the jailhouse he saw the tethered horse and recognised the brand. When he walked in he nodded to the cowman, went to his desk to be seated as he said, 'Let me guess. Jeff Mesa . . .'

Dodge nodded, his perpetually squinted eyes gravely considered the constable. 'That was a damfool thing to do,' he said quietly. 'I know — folks aren't real fond of Jeff, but right now that don't matter. What matters is that you're takin' the side of the priest an' his mongrel bulls. Jeff'll make certain every cowman within ridin' distance hears about that.' Dodge's grave pronouncement was interrupted by a mosquito that bit him on the back of the neck. He killed it and scratched vigorously for a moment before continuing.

'Elrey, I been holdin' back. Hell, if them bulls bred our cows it's done by now, an' it can't be un-done. But no one can tell until nine months from now what their mammy cows is goin' to calve out, but they'll worry a lot an' that means they'll make damned sure it don't never happen again.'

Elrey explained about the priest's agreement to get rid of his longhorns, and that answered a question Dodge'd had in mind since reaching town; the partially-completed big, stout corral north of town.

He tipped back his hat to reveal a shockingly white forehead. 'You figure to corral them bulls this close to town?' Dodge was shaking his head before Elrey spoke. After he spoke the old cowman with the slitted eyes stopped his negative head-wagging.

'Chief Baca said to put it up there, Dodge. He's said to be as good a stockman as there is in the country.'

Dodge commented drily. 'He is. An' he rides for me, Elrey. That sort of complicates things.'

'How?'

'Well, to commence with, the other ranchers will wonder about me lettin' one of my riders take the side of the priest. For another thing, Chief never said a word to me about any of this, an' I don't like that.'

Elrey considered his clasped hands atop the desk. 'Does workin' for you include nights? Because if it don't, that's when he comes to town. He's sparking a widow down in Mex town, an' that's when we've talked.'

Dodge too was silent for a thoughtful few moments. He was a hard, resourceful, but fair man. What he had just heard about one of his riders did not anger him, but it certainly annoyed him. The matter had nothing to do with Chief coming to town on his own time, the issue was what he had done to help friends of the priest while he was on his own, an act any cowman would view as betrayal.

The older man sighed, shoved out warped legs and stared solemnly at his boots. 'This damned mess is gettin' more difficult by the day,' he mused aloud.

Elrey turned placating. 'You said the priest should have time to get rid of the longhorns. Dodge, he needs more time. He's trying an' I'll do everything I can to help him. My interest isn't you stockmen or the priest; my interest is to prevent a damned war.'

Dodge looked up. 'What war?'

'What Jeff did yesterday, or whenever he did it, could be the beginning of a plan to kill the priest's bulls. From your side of the fence that most likely seems like the best idea. From my side of the fence it don't. Everyone who knows Father Cross likes him. The folks in Mex town love him. You or Jeff or someone else starts killing his cattle and the Mexicans won't like it one bit. They'll see it as rich stockmen picking on one of their own.'

Plummer returned to studying his boots. After a while he said, 'One thing you told me true; the cows are all bred back by now.' Plummer arose not looking very happy. 'I can't speak for Jeff Mesa, but all right, I'll go among the others and tell them you'n the priest are going to get the damned bulls off the range. But Elrey, that may not be enough.'

After Dodge Plummer departed Elrey stood in front of one of his small roadway barred windows looking out.

When a man had been supporting the law long enough, he developed a kind of instinct about trouble. Elrey's instinct told him it was coming as sure as night followed day.

He didn't go up to Kelly's place for his usual nightcap, he walked the full length of town northward, and past where duckboards ended until he could see the silhouette of the partially completed corral.

He was impressed. He could not see over the topmost log stringers and he was almost six feet tall. The posts would not budge when he threw his weight against them. They were tamped three feet into the ground and were set at four foot intervals. He had never seen such a strong corral.

It was actually two corrals, the second one was some distance from where massive gate posts showed where the entrance would be. The second corral was not as large as the main corral.

Another thing that impressed him

was the amount of work that had been accomplished in one day. He was leaning there speculating about the dedication of the priest's parishioners, who had worked so hard so long, when a soft voice said, 'It is better than I expected.'

Chief Baca strode close and also leaned to judge the work. Elrey had no difficulty imagining why Baca was in Coyanosa tonight. But remembering Dodge Plummer's reaction to his tophand's behaviour he felt compelled to mention Plummer's visit.

Chief shrugged. 'I didn't tell him. He would find out. Will he fire me?' Another shrug as Chief turned his engaging smile on Elrey Austin. 'I don't think so. I know him very well. We share a fondness; we have both grown old with cattle, believe the same way. Well, if he fires me I can then spend all my time in town.'

Chief laughed, more to himself than for the benefit of his companion, and reverted to his earlier statement, 'How did they get it so well built in one day?'

Elrey mentioned his earlier thoughts. 'For the priest.'

Chief nodded. 'They could finish it tomorrow.'

'Yeah . . . Chief, what happens next?'

'I get some help and start rounding up trinity bulls. Cows too if they come along, but the stockmen don't care about longhorn cows, just the bulls.'

'Who will help you? It's one hell of a big range.'

'*Compañeros*. A few others. Maybe even the priest, but I don't think so. It's hard work for long hours.'

'And dangerous,' Elrey said.

Baca shook his head. 'Not very dangerous. If it's done right it won't be dangerous at all, and I aim to see that it is done right.'

Chief leaned off the massive logs to methodically roll and light a cigarette. He exhaled looking at the night sky. 'Elrey, I am much older than you. I am old enough to know that before the bulls it was something else and that after the bulls it will continue to be something else. I'll tell you what I've wondered over the years — rangeriding give a man lots of time to think — people make things; houses, towns, roads. Everything they make means they must maintain them. When they cut a forest to make buildings they have to ever after paint or oil or patch their buildings. The same when they make roads; they have to go out from time to time and keep up their roads.'

Chief Baca put his winsome smile on Elrey again. 'They bring in longhorns at first, then no longer need that kind of cattle so they breed-up for beef quality and hate longhorns.

'They shoot them, run them off. They get mad at people who keep longhorns. Do you see? When you change something what you really are doing is making certain that your change will make you the slave of your change. Today it is the holy father's bulls, tomorrow when the bulls are gone it will be something else. It will always be something.'

Elrey who hadn't been expecting any of this, leaned on the corral gazing as far as the ghostly silhouettes of star-framed mountains.

Chief slapped him lightly on the shoulder and said one more thing before walking back in the direction of the widow's house. 'Two days. I'll come back in two days. If the corral is ready, then we will do what is next.'

It did not occur to Elrey until Baca was gone that he hadn't mentioned his run-in with Jeff Mesa. It did not right then seem important. He strolled back to the hotel with a quiet, nearly lightless town, around him. He bedded down trying to make sense of what Baca had said. Before falling asleep he began to understand. He wondered if other men had not had those same thoughts and had perhaps been better able to put them into words.

The following morning Father Cross came to see him at the jailhouse. His robe was soiled, his hands were swollen and scabbed over, and although he had probably slept well the previous night, he looked tired.

The priest made a joke of that. It was much harder digging in parched ground than it was being on one's knees in the church chapel.

Elrey thought he was working too hard at something he had probably never done before, but did not mention this. The Little Mule of Mission San Angelo was not a man to be even mildly scolded about working.

Two rangeriders had passed on their way to town while Father Cross's Mex town labourers were out yonder and had taunted them. Father Cross thought that by now the rangemen were becoming troublesome and might become more so. But he had no intention of telling his workers to bring weapons to the corral with them.

He wanted Elrey to know there might be trouble at the corral, something Elrey nodded unhappily about. He should have anticipated it, what with the corral so close to town and the north-south roadway.

'I'll pass word around, Father. Chief Baca was in town last night. He'll be back in two days to see if you're finished.'

The little priest was in the doorway when he replied. 'We will be finished tomorrow, and Elrey, I doubt if there has ever been bulls stout enough to get out once they're in our corral.'

Elrey hoped with all his heart that the priest was right.

In the late afternoon Feliciano Cortez appeared in town with three hired riders. He left the rangemen over at the general store with his list, crossed to the jailhouse and walked in shaking off sweat. Spring was fast fading, summer was in the wings.

Feliciano had a dumpy little jovial wife and nine children, an admirable record for a man who had been married eight years.

He had the olive complexion of a *gachupin*, was no more than average height with a tendency to thicken. He was wealthy, owned thousands of deeded acres and controlled as many more through hereditary use. He was a business man, and a very good one, but he was also somewhat like Dodge Plummer in his tolerance.

Except where the trinity bulls were concerned.

He knew of Elrey's brawl with Jeff Mesa and repeated what Elrey had told Mesa almost word for word. When he had done this he said, 'He's hard to get along with. No one knows that better'n I do. Our land adjoins for twenty miles, but he is right about those bulls, and Elrey. I want to tell you — if you make a fight with Mesa, you will make a fight with me and the others.'

Elrey blew out a ragged breath. That son of a bitch Jeff Mesa must have done nothing the last couple of days but ride around stirring up the stockmen, an undertaking of no small importance since all the ranches were separated by many miles.

'Felix, I didn't make that fight, Jeff did.'

'You threatened him?'

'I told him if he killed any more of Father Cross's bulls I'd come looking for him, after he told me he'd offered a cartwheel to his riders if they shot trinity bulls.'

'Well; you won't shoot them, and they are . . . '

'And neither will Jeff, if I find out. I'll tell you what I told Dodge: Father Cross needs more time. Dodge agreed he should have it. Felix, killing his bulls will get Mex town fired up for a war. You understand? It's not the damned bulls, it's a war I want to prevent.'

Cortez scoffed. 'There won't be a war. But if there was the men from Mex town wouldn't stand a chance against the cattlemen and their riders.'

Elrey ignored that. 'The priest needs a few more days. He's agreed to sell his longhorns.' Before Cortez could bring up the topic Mesa had mentioned, Elrey told him Chief Baca was going to take care of rounding up and driving the trinity bulls.

Cortez's black brows climbed upwards. 'Does Dodge know this?'

'By now he most likely does.'

'He won't like it, Elrey. He won't like it at all and neither would I. Chief is a rangeman. His job is to . . . '

'Felix, damn it, I just told you I'm walking on eggs to prevent this from becoming a war. Baca is the only man I know who just might bring those damned bulls off the range.'

Feliciano Cortez fell to examining the crown of the hat he held in his lap. Elrey could tell from the man's profile, Cortez was troubled, which was understandable, but Elrey had his own position and proved it by asking a question.

'Will you keep your men from shooting the bulls?'

Cortez got slowly to his feet, dropped the hat on the back of his head and replied slowly. 'A week. I will say and do nothing for one week starting today

. . . But Jeff won't. He hates you now.'

Elrey also arose as he drily said, 'We were never friends.'

Cortez left the office on his way across the roadway where his riders were waiting. Elrey watched from the window. Normally stockmen treated their riders to a drink at the saloon on their way out of town. Feliciano Cortez did not even turn his head as he led his men back the way they had come.

Elrey went to the middle of the dusty road to look northward. At least eight men were out there under a pitiless sun working with Father Cross. The corral was nearing completion. Elrey continued in the direction of Kelly's cantina, and, as had happened often lately, he arrived up there with only some old men in a far corner and Jawn swabbing glasses behind his bar.

Kelly did not give the constable a chance. He moved to draw off a glass of beer as he said, 'Well, everyone knows what that elephant corral is for above town.'

Elrey accepted the beer as he replied. 'It was never a secret, Jawn.'

'It's crazy. That damned thing will stand empty up there for fifty years. Even Chief Baca can't round up all the trinity bulls and get them down here in the corral. Maybe even the Angel Gabriel couldn't do it.'

Elrey half-emptied his glass and gazed thoughtfully at Jawn Kelly. 'Chief Baca don't need the Angel Gabriel, he needs you'n me to help bring the bulls in.'

Jawn's very blue eyes steadily widened. 'Me an' you? You got any idea what bringin' that bunch in will amount to? Me? Elrey, I haven't even been on a horse in twelve years.'

'About as long since you've been at Mass, Jawn?'

For a moment the implication did not register, then Jawn Kelly's face darkened. 'That don't have a damned thing to do with . . .'

'Father Cross has done more for Coyanosa since he's been here than you'n I'll most likely ever do. He needs help.'

'You help him then,' Jawn said, and stamped back to his bucket of greasy water to pick out a glass and begin to furiously polish it.

Elrey finished his beer, placed a coin beside the glass, gazed a moment at the upset glass-polisher then walked out of the saloon.

At supper that evening Elrey was finishing a meal when Jawn walked in, glared at the cafeman and sank down hard next to the constable. He snapped his order at the bewildered cafeman, then leaned and turned to say, 'You got any idea how old I am?'

Elrey did not even look up from his meal. 'As old as Chief Baca?'

Jawn glowered and a vein in the side of his neck swelled. He was ten years younger than Chief Baca. It had been a good guess by the constable.

Kelly tried a fresh approach. 'I got a business to run. For Chriz'sake you know what you're asking?'

Elrey did not answer until he was standing, placing coins beside his plate, then as he turned to depart he made a remark even the cafeman heard.

'Language like that will set you to roasting in hell, Jawn. I don't know much about salvation, but havin' a priest on your side can't hurt.'

6

Coyanosa In Turmoil

Something occurred Elrey was a while figuring out. When he got down to the cafe for breakfast the saloonman was not there and did not arrive although Elrey dawdled over his coffee. He asked the cafeman if Jawn had eaten earlier and got a sullen wag of the head. The cafeman had a poor disposition at best; early mornings it was as bad as it would be all day.

Elrey went up to the saloon. Its spindle doors were secured from the outside by a brass lock as large as a man's fist.

Coyanosa did not have a medical doctor. It had a midwife who, at times cured boils, knife wounds and the rare gunshot wound, along with galls on the backs of horses, splints when they could be cured which was not often, and collar sores. Elrey encountered her in front of the general store and asked if Jawn Kelly was sick.

She did not know. If he was he had not come to her nor had she heard of him being ill.

He was at the saddle and harness shop, a small, fragrant, dark building when someone told him there was a woman down at his office.

He walked in, Carmen Bohorquez flashed a dazzling smile and asked in Spanish how he was. He replied in the same language that he was well enough, and enquired what he could do for the handsome widow.

She seemed amused about something as she swung back to English. 'He took two men from town. Jawn Kelly and an old stringbean of a *vaquero* named Amos Sanchez.'

'Who — what are you talking about?'

The dazzling smile widened. 'Ramon Baca. He spent the night in town and took those two when he rode away about three o'clock this morning.'

Elrey had a glimmer. He eased back in his chair eyeing the widow Borhorquez. 'The trinity bulls?'

She nodded. 'He came after dark last night. I fed him. *Señor* Plummer let him have all his riders, and there are others waiting five miles out. I walked to the bull corral with him last night. He was pleased with it. I am to tell the holy father, and you, that no one is to go near the corral for maybe two, three days. No dogs. He said particularly no dogs, no children, no people at all. *Comprende?*'

Elrey sat gazing at the widow. 'Why didn't he let me know?'

She shrugged round shoulders, and arose to say she had to find the priest.

Elrey stopped her in the doorway. 'It's not a secret, is it?'

She shrugged again. 'No, but if the people in town don't know, they won't go out there to watch, will they?' She closed the door.

Elrey sat a while looking at the far wall. He thought Baca should have told him. It hadn't been mentioned between them and, in fact, now it no longer mattered. Events would take their own course.

He walked up the north side of Coyanosa's wide main thoroughfare and was caught by the men who operated the stage-stop, a large, massive Irishman named Cullough, who had dropped the Mc years earlier. He told Elrey there was a rumour floating around town that Jawn Kelly had hired a horse and had left town in the dark of the previous night, or early morning; the rumour had it that Jawn had a secret love and was going to go somewhere and be married.

Elrey controlled his amusement. Cullough must surely have heard Jawn Kelly's opinion of women over the years, everyone else had. He gave a small shrug and said, 'Who knows?' in Spanish, continued up to the north end of town and stood in shade up there gazing out where the completed corral stood.

Chief must have wished to say nothing about what he was up to, or perhaps he'd decided the people in town would be curious if they knew what was coming and, as he'd told the handsome widow, he did not want people anywhere near the corrals, which was reasonable. If he and his riders spent days locating and easing the cattle ahead, the last thing they would want was a crowd of noisy spectators when the bulls came into sight. *If* they came into sight.

A genuine secret in a place like Coyanosa was only slightly longer spreading than half a secret. By mid-day everyone knew and most other topics were ignored for the villagers to engage in speculation, even betting money one way or another about the trinity bulls.

When Elrey was approached he repeated the admonition that no one was to go out to the corral and their dogs were to be kept quiet. What the womenfolk thought was less important to the men than the fact that the saloon was closed and padlocked.

Elrey was down at the smithy when the perpetually worried, sniffing proprietor of the general store found him and said there was something odd going on. There was no sign of Jawn Kelly and one of his Mexican customers said Kelly and a rawhide-built old *vaquero* named Amos Sanchez had been seen stealthily riding out of town several hours before sunrise.

The sniffing storekeeper had his own opinion which was that local merchant or not, Jawn Kelly had left town with two other Mexicans and assuredly they were going to meet that band of renegades operating somewhere up north, and lead them back to Coyanosa.

Even the rawboned lanky blacksmith scowled at the storekeeper, turned his back and went to work shoeing one of Elrey's horses.

Elrey leaned in the sooty little shady shop regarding the storekeeper, who had already made him waste one hot day. 'Jawn Kelly went for a ride with a couple of friends. That's all.'

'At two in the morning armed to the teeth — with two companions?'

Elrey made a forced smile. 'Everyone rides out accordin' to their own ideas. Lots of people ride out before sunrise to avoid the heat. And going armed is common. Don't worry so much.'

The merchant scuttled back the way he had come when Elrey turned his back on him; he was a long way from being placated.

The blacksmith spoke around shoeing nails between his lips. 'One time years back I went wood cutting with him. He leaned his axe against a tree to rest, an' when he went to pick it up a coiled rattlesnake made its racket fifty feet away . . . He fainted; took me fifteen minutes dousing with water to fetch him around.'

Elrey led the freshly shod horse to

the corral behind the jailhouse where he kept two saddle animals.

He was in the office when the way-station boss walked in out of the still cool morning. His name was Pat Cullough, he was big-boned, muscled-up and usually calm. This time as he eased down on a bench he said, 'A driver on one of the southbound coaches from up around Guadalupe come in a while ago. I thought you might want to know; renegades raided two remote cow outfits, killed everyone and fired the buildings. The soldiers from up there went after them.' Cullough was long faced. 'That garrison up there is foot soldiers.'

Elrey understood the implication. He also knew that fleeing renegades had ten different directions at their disposal, which made the odds very high that they had not fled southeasterly down where Coyanosa was. Still, he told the stager he'd alert men around town, and after Cullough departed Elrey dug out his bottle, swallowed twice and left the jailhouse to pass word among merchants and other townsmen that he thought it might be a good idea to activate the local vigilantes.

It only belatedly occurred to him that Chief Baca and his roundup riders would be up-country looking for bulls; they could very easily be directly in the path of the band of killers.

If they were riding strung out, the customary way when searching for cattle, they would be easy targets. If they were riding in a party of maybe as many as fifteen men, even a superior number of renegades would hesitate to start a fight. Marauding renegades killed from ambush, struck without warning and disappeared in darkness, they did not fight pitched battles.

He thought about riding in search of Baca and his men; the difficulty with that was Elrey had no idea which way the bull hunters had gone and as immense as the land was, more than a thousand miles of range, his chance of finding them was down to just about zero.

It irritated him again that Chief Baca had been so closed-mouthed.

He walked out to the bull corral and leaned in its shade, arrived at a decision, returned to town and asked the blacksmith to ride to the Plummer place, now evidently stripped of its riders, and warn Dodge.

The blacksmith was willing. Not happy but willing.

After listening to Elrey he sardonically said, 'Well, that damned storekeeper and his fits could be right this time, eh?'

Elrey agreed, but avoided the general store as he went through town passing the news from Cullough. He might as well have gone to the general store first. He was back in his office in mid-afternoon when the storekeeper came scuttling over, apron rolled up and tucked into the waistband of his trousers, eyes wide and nose twitching from irregular sniffs.

'I told you,' he said in his nasal, high-pitched voice. 'You turned your back on me an' I told you. Elrey, you got to send for the army. There could be a hunnert of 'em.'

Elrey asked what army? The nearest army camp was southeast forty-five miles. It was from this emplacement the cavalrymen had ridden to intercept the border jumpers. It would take a rider almost a full day to get down there and, assuming soldiers were there and not out chasing troublemakers, it would require another day, maybe two days, for them to reach Coyanosa.

But he did agree someone should go down there and the storekeeper volunteered his clerk, a young man who had once been a rangerider.

Before Elrey could concur the storekeeper fled back across to his store.

Elrey watched the blacksmith leave town on a leggy, rawboned, big roman-nosed horse that had toughness built into every line of his body.

That still left Chief Baca and his riders.

Believing it would be hopeless, Elrey nevertheless dragooned a pair of *vaqueros* from Mex town. He told them everything he knew and pointed them in what he assumed would be the right direction.

They left Coyanosa with rising heat over the land, and in town, rising fear along with it.

The big, stout corral north of town which had been the butt of subtle and not so subtle ridicule, was replaced by the more threatening rumour of raiders, one of those bands of hard-riding murderers who had replaced Apaches as the most feared scourge of the Territory.

Elrey went down to the widow Bohorquez's residence to see if she had heard anything. She hadn't, but she fed Elrey and a trifle shyly talked about Chief Baca, using his given name of Ramon.

She promised to seek the constable at

once if she picked up any information in Mex town, the best source, and Elrey returned to his office where it was ten degrees cooler than the roadway.

The blacksmith returned in late afternoon, Dodge Plummer came with him and brought along his chore boy, a young Mexican barely into his teens. He told Elrey, after he had lambasted Chief Baca for not telling him he had been working to help the priest, that Baca had asked him point-blank if he could use the hired riders to find and drive the trinity bulls.

Dodge sat broodingly in the jailhouse office. 'I let him have 'em. What the hell, them bulls had to be got off the range, didn't they? An' Chief's the best man in the country to do it.'

Elrey showed no expression about the old cowman's defensive attitude. He asked him if he knew a man named Amos Sanchez. Dodge inclined his head. 'Tall, scrawny feller near my age.' He suddenly widened his gaze. 'Chief took Amos with him?'

'And Jawn Kelly.'

Plummer stared for a moment, then nodded grudgingly. 'Amos is tough. Old as dirt — or me — but tough and *coyote* . . . Jawn Kelly? Well, I don't know whether he'll be any good or not, but sweatin' off ten pounds will maybe make him live longer . . . Unless they get caught out by them renegades. You heard any more about 'em?'

'No, but it don't pay to take chances, does it?

Dodge agreed. 'Nope, with no one left at the ranch but me'n the chore-boy, if they raid the place at least the lad an' I'll survive.'

Dodge shifted in his chair. 'I've seen what they leave. Quite a few times; they shoot anythin' that moves. They drink anything they find, then they really go to work, torturin' folks if they figure there's hidden money or such like. Elrey, I'm here to tell you damned In'ians could learn about cruelty from men like that. Messicans, sometimes 'breed In'ians, white scum of every stinkin' hell-hole of a border town.'

Elrey and Dodge Plummer went over to the cafe with dusk settling. There were other diners as well as the grumpy, garrulous cafeman. The place was as silent as a grave.

Later, going back to the jailhouse office because the saloon was closed, Elrey handed Dodge Plummer his bottle. The older man nursed it between swallows as though there was no one else in the room. Elrey cleared his throat. Dodge jerked out of a bitter reverie and handed over the bottle as he said, 'You know, years back when we heard one of them bands was in the country we didn't wait, didn't bother with the army, everyone got astride an' we run 'em down no matter how long it took . . . Left 'em where they fell for the buzzards. If they give up, we hung 'em from the nearest tree . . . Never brought back a single one. Elrey, times was better then. Folks knew right from wrong, they didn't need no constables or marshals or sheriffs.'

Elrey put the bottle away and was leaning to arise when a sweaty pair of exhausted-looking Mexicans walked in out of the darkness. They ignored Dodge and told Elrey they had changed horses twice at outlying ranches in order to make the best time, and they had not found Ramon Baca or any of his riders. But they had found someone else about fifteen miles northeast of the Plummer yard, a badly wounded gringo who smelled to high heaven, dirty, unshaven, half delirious. He told them he had been shot by soldiers after a raid on an outlying ranch in the Guadalupe country. He had a bottle of whiskey his friends had left when they took his horse and raced away. He laughed as he told them of the killings. He had died in the middle of a burst of laughter.

They left him where he died and came back to town. Dodge said. 'West? They run west?'

The vaqueros repeated that this was what the dying renegade had said.

Dodge got to his feet. For the first

time since he had arrived in town, his expression was no longer brooding and resigned. 'I'll find the lad an' take him back to the ranch with me . . . West is the wrong direction for me — an' for Coyanosa.'

After the old cowman departed Elrey questioned the vaqueros. There was not much they could tell him they had not already said, but they filled in a few minor details, such as the appearance of the dying renegade, and the bad condition of the only gun his companions had left with him, which they had not bothered to bring back.

After the vaqueros left Elrey wondered if Chief Baca's riders were far enough northward to be intercepted by renegades fleeing westerly. It did not seem probable; they had left in the morning, early, it would require a lot of riding to even get near the Guadalupe country. If that abandoned dying man had been found late today, it probably meant the renegades had fled west long before anyone from the

Coyanosa country had gotten that far north.

Elrey went to bed worried but not nearly as anxious as he had been before the vaqueros returned. There was no guarantee those murderers would still not head down into the Coyanosa country, but if they did, it would not be for a while. Men riding west across open country would cover a lot of ground, more ground if they knew soldiers were after them.

Further, fugitives fleeing west with soldiers behind them were unlikely to even change course for many miles.

Elrey slept well. Before dawn as he was cleaning up out back at the wash house, he returned to his earlier thoughts about Chief Baca and his bull hunters. He needed answers to several questions but the man who could give them was a long way off hunting wild bulls.

It still annoyed him that Baca had not taken him into his confidence . . . unless of course Baca, seeing the completed corral, decided on the spur of the moment to begin his miles deep and days long roundup.

Which was exactly what had happened.

7

No Sleep This Night

Coyanosa was alive with rumours, understandable given the scares and speculations which were rife. Elrey heard some of them when he went around the town talking to merchants and others who belonged to the vigilance committee.

This too, heightened the tension. Business fell off and if the saloon hadn't been closed, it might have also lost trade, although that was problematical.

For two days following the raider-scare people were relieved and worried at the same time. With just cause; several of the rumours had to do with what happened to villages attacked by large roving bands of renegades, and here the oldtimers around town had a field day recalling hair-raising, bloody

111

tales of such raids.

Elrey's office had a stream of visitors, mostly of two varieties; the badly frightened needing reassurance, and heavily armed men seeking coordination from the local lawman concerning positions and tactics if the town was attacked.

This latter problem Elrey resolved quite simply. Every vigilante in town was to stay close, not go wandering beyond town limits. They were to sleep with weapons at hand. If the town were attacked, they were to fight as was customary, from lofts, behind buildings, from alleyways, and to keep moving as they fought, the tactic to be simply to catch raiders from both sides of the main road, and if that was not practical, to use every deceptive tactic Indians used to kill without being killed.

Elrey gave this advice even after it was generally known the Guadalupe raiders were fleeing westerly with the army in pursuit.

He personally felt fairly certain there

would be no attack. His reason for heightening the posture of defence was twofold. It would keep people in town, away from the big corral north of town, and it would provide townsmen with something to occupy their time.

As it turned out, his ideas were sound but for the wrong reasons.

He talked to Cullough out front of the palisaded corralyard of the way-station. The only fresh news his drivers had brought was what everyone already knew; the army was in pursuit of the raiders. Cullough looked stonily at the constable as he said this. 'Them runnin' as fast as they can, most likely on stolen, fresh horses, an' them troopers up north marching on foot or ridin' in wagons.'

Elrey went over to the gunshop where the proprietor was sweating and the sun had only been up a couple of hours. The gunsmith was an old man. He jutted his jaw Indian-fashion in the direction of stacks of leaning and hanging weapons, each with a small tag attached to it. 'They been settin' on a mantle or stood up in a closet for five years. All of a sudden the fellers who own 'em come runnin' in here demandin' to have their guns worked on and finished by sundown.'

Elrey commiserated. 'It's better'n just whittlin' out new stocks and watching folks go by in the roadway without comin' in.'

To this the old man agreed while mopping sweat off his bald head with a limp old faded blue bandana. 'For a fact, Constable — only I'd like it better if everyone wasn't in such a rush. Then I could spread the work out over two, three months.' The old man pocketed his bandana and looked directly at Elrey as he resumed speaking. 'All the jabberin' around town don't amount to a hill of beans. Folks forget us oldtimers had this kind of trouble every few months, an' we didn't go runnin' around like chickens with their heads chopped off. We kept a big pile of dry wood several places a couple miles out, and had young feller out there with a sulphur match and a spyglass.

'The moment they saw a band of hard-riders comin' our way, they fired the wood. By the time the raiders got close, there was a gun out every window, atop most roofs, in sheds and behind whatever a man could find to get behind. We wasn't never surprised.'

'In darkness?' Elrey asked a little sceptically.

'In darkness you could hear 'em coming a long time before you seen 'em. You suspicioned something, you got down on your belly and put your ear to the ground. A lot of fast-movin' horses make noise that carries in the ground for one hell of a distance.'

Elrey eyed the racked rifles and carbines, even a scattering of shotguns, some with two barrels, some long and some sawed off. He left the gunsmith at his work and walked down the east side of the roadway paying calls on merchants, but he bypassed the general store, and ended up down near the smithy before crossing over and doing the same thing on the west side of the road.

Beyond that there was little he could do but wait, which was exactly what everyone else was doing.

Time passed slowly, heat kept people in doors for better than half the day, and Coyanosa had the appearance of a ghost town for much of the time.

But as happened with all waiting, there eventually came an end to it. This happened the third day with heat waves obscuring distances and making stationary or moving objects appear to be detached from the ground.

In the early evening a horseman appeared to the northeast. He halted over there, visible from town, sat still gazing in the direction of Coyanosa. He was too distant to be recognised as anyone local, if indeed he was, and that set the sniffing storekeeper to hunt down Elrey and tell him excitedly that a renegade scout was a half mile or such a matter northeast of town sitting his horse while he calmly figured out the best way to attack.

The merchant left Elrey and scuttled around town bearing the same tale. By the time the horseman raised his left hand to ride closer, vigilantes were secreted every imaginable place with their weapons.

Elrey stood over in front of the gun works near the upper end of town, watching that mysterious rider. When the man started toward town at a dead walk, Elrey heard the old gunsmith behind him make a snort. The old man said, 'One gawddamned rider's got the whole town scairt peeless. He ain't no more a renegade then I am. Constable, you recognise him?'

Elrey could see the rider fairly well, heat haze notwithstanding, but could not identify him. 'Who?' he asked the gunsmith and got a disgusted retort.

'Amos Sanchez for Chriz'sake. He's lived here all his life.' The old man stamped back into his shop.

Elrey, who knew Amos Sanchez to

nod to, leaned and waited until he was sure, then turned and called along the hushed, empty roadway, for no one to show a weapon. That the rider lived in Coyanosa.

By the time the lean horseman reached those massive log gates of the priest's corral and dismounted to open them wide and prop them in place, others had recognised him.

Men appeared on both sides of the roadway holding slack weapons. Some, too embarrassed, simply slunk to their homes or shops and put up the guns.

Amos Sanchez got the wide gates propped, did not so much as look back as he mounted and rode slowly back the way he had come until heat haze blurred him almost into extinction.

Coyanosa had residents whose early lives had been spent with cattle. Like Elrey they guessed why Sanchez had appeared and disappeared. Two hours later, with dusk thickening, they heard the noise and eventually caught the scent of driven cattle.

Elrey passed word no one was to go out there.

The cattle arrived, not very many, maybe twelve to fifteen head, bawling their protest every step of the way and raising pungent dust through which what looked to be no more than four or five riders rode at a dead walk easing the critters in the direction of the gate.

It went off like clockwork, which did not surprise anyone who had worked up-graded cows; they were docile enough to obey horsemen with little trouble even though each cow was bulling hard which, under most circumstances, made them cranky and troublesome. But these were stubby-legged grade Herefords.

They were corralled without difficulty, pushed on through to the smaller corral and left. Their racket diminished; they had been driven a long distance for critters with heavy bodies and short legs. They would need water tomorrow. As for feed, that too, if they were corralled for any length of time.

Elrey heard someone approaching and turned. It was the way-station boss, Pat Cullough. Behind him was the town blacksmith. They stood and watched in silence as the gate was closed on the cows and the riders turned back the way they had come without so much as a look in the direction of town.

The blacksmith, a spare man with words, made a dry comment. 'He's got 'em disciplined. I've known Baca fifteen years. Never could figure out why Plummer or some stockman didn't hire him on as rangeboss.'

Pat Cullough provided an answer. 'He's told me couple times he don't want the responsibility; he just wants freedom with a good horse under him.'

The riders faded into settling darkness, the cows bawled some, probably would continue to do it intermittently all night, but as Elrey told the men behind him, it would not be long before they knew whether Chief Baca could do what a lot of sceptics doubted that anyone could accomplish, drive wild longhorn bulls.

The following morning the sniffing storekeeper was the recipient of heavy-handed ridicule for spreading an alarm about raiders. The merchant remained in his store making feeble excuses.

Several humanitarians wanted to know if they couldn't tank up a water wagon and haul a trough out there for the cows. The decision was left to Elrey. His quandary was that he had no idea where the bulls were. If he was still out there watering the bulling cows when the bulls appeared, everything would be spoiled.

He allowed the wagon to be filled and left with the tongue on the ground. The cows would be uncomfortable but it couldn't be helped.

An enterprising teenager got atop the roof of his home, ignored the anxious, and eventually angry yells of his mother to get down from there, and, with his father's brass spyglass, sat in the heat watching for dust.

Other watchers elsewhere throughout

Coyanosa kept the vigil. It was a very long, hot day. The remarks about the saloon being closed became more noticeably acerbic as time passed.

It was widely known that Jawn Kelly was with Baca's riders, and while this was considered admirable the first day or two, by the fourth day it was widely held that the saloonman would have served his community better by minding his business in town, and anyway, if Jawn had once been a rider, that had been a long while back and he therefore had no business riding on a dangerous mission with men who spent all their waking moments in the saddle.

Particularly now that summer was fully on the land. As punky as Jawn Kelly was, he could suffer a heart seizure, then just who the hell would unlock and operate the damned saloon?

Coyanosa had been in a state of anxiety for longer than anyone could remember. Elrey had to be tactful, which was foreign to his nature. He was a straightforward individual. This period taught him something about restraint. Whether he would remember in the years ahead was something else, but with the penning of the bulling cows people became less critical of what had been transpiring, and had become caught up in speculation and wagers: Would the wild bulls come or wouldn't they?

Those two vaqueros from Mex town volunteered to ride forth and join Baca's riders. Elrey had to be careful how he worded his refusal. Chief Baca was in charge out yonder. All he had required of the townsfolk was that they stay clear and keep their dogs quiet, which was not very much to ask in comparison to the days of hardship Baca and his riders had put in.

The vaqueros, young though they were, understood and left the jailhouse still in good spirits.

Elrey got a surprise. It was dark after supper, the lad with the spyglass had climbed down for supper. Even if he remained at his elevated perch darkness

123

would have prevented him from seeing anything.

Others around town who were vigilant were also unprepared when Elrey, up near the north end of town, heard the first challenging bellow.

He did not move. Other than that one bawl he heard nothing, but he knew the fighting bawl of a bull when he heard it. This particular animal was deep-throated and thunderous when he bellowed.

Several dogs barked. Elrey swore, hoping those sounds would not carry far.

There were other bellows. They seemed to be moving forward in an irregular half circle. He made that judgement based on the sounds.

Others also heard the trumpeting. Slowly people appeared on both sides of the dark roadway. Two barking dogs were abruptly silenced. A third one yipped in either fright or pain, probably the latter, when its owner drove it into silence.

A small robed figure appeared silently beside the constable clutching his large Cross in both hands. He whispered something in Spanish which Elrey did not understand, then became silent as the actual sound of many large animals reverberated through the night.

Coyanosa was silent, people did as the constable had done, they gauged, movement from sounds. It appeared to be a large herd of heavy animals. Elrey hoped hard it would be many bulls.

The bellowing encouraged some answering bawls from the bulling cows inside the corral, and that started the bulls which could be heard but not seen, to increase their rush toward the scent that over-rode every other consideration, even possible danger, in their small minds.

The old gunsmith materialised without his apron and softly said, 'Fellers, the best place to get yourselves ground into mincemeat right now would be between them bulls an' them bullin' cows.' He chuckled.

The noise increased until it resembled the thunderous rush of buffalo. The bulls, following scent, crashed into the corral and its gate posts in their fight to reach the cows. There was not a sound from horsemen out there. Chief Baca had never allowed his riders to do more than keep the longhorns heading in roughly the correct direction, and that was accomplished from a distance.

He and his men still remained far back, at least a quarter of a mile until they could hear the bulls crashing into the corral, then Chief called to Amos Sanchez in Spanish to go southward, far below the bulls and come north until he could see they were all in the corral, then he was to dash in, slam the gates and chain them.

Red-faced Boss Cleaver, riding stirrup with Baca, let fly with a squirt of molasses-cured and straightened in the saddle with a smile. 'I told you, Chief, if you lived right it would work.'

Baca replied with his head cocked to the sounds by the corral. 'I always lived right, Boss. You know that. Except now an' then.'

Riders converged at a dead walk until they were stirrup to stirrup, and continued in the direction of the corral.

There was some talk, mostly hopeful, but not very much. Jawn Kelly was sore in places he did not even know he had, but he was a proud man; he could have been dragged behind wild horses and still not allow the others to know how he had suffered these last days. As someone had said, Jawn Kelly would work off ten pounds. He did that, and a little more.

They heard the gates slam and chains rattle before Baca raised his left hand and squeezed his horse. The others rode with him. The racket changed as the fighting longhorns discovered that they had been trapped. They repeatedly hurled themselves at the corral. Sounds of groaning wood could be heard to the far end of Coyanosa.

The bellowing changed in timbre and loudness. Father Cross's critters were challenging the world. He moved a little closer to Elrey. 'If they break out,' he murmured, and the hard old gunsmith answered him curtly.

'They'll come down through town knockin' down everythin' in their path. I've seen it happen. There's nothin' as blind crazy as longhorn bulls on the prod.'

The priest crossed himself which the other men did not notice, they were straining to see out yonder and were gauging every sound when bulls tried to break out of the massive corral.

8

The Next Day

The wild bulls' earlier compelling interest in bulling cows was forgotten when they discovered they had been trapped.

Their bellowing awakened the soundest sleeper in Coyanosa. They repeatedly hurled themselves against the massive corral, boards creaked and posts groaned.

For the onlookers in town it was a time of anxiety; no one knew whether the corral would hold them or not, and if it did not, as the gunsmith had said, enraged fighting bulls charged anything they saw, moving or still. In a blood-rage those descendants of Spanish fighting bulls hurled themselves at whatever object they encountered. As he had also mentioned, that many bulls would cause havoc in a town if they charged through it.

Father Cross was rooted beside Elrey Austin. Others on both sides of the dark roadway were also silent and motionless and finally, probably with no one to prevent it now that the town was expecting the worst out front along the roadway, town dogs began barking their heads off.

It was a nightmare. At any moment the combined charge of so many big, strong fighting bulls might smash their way out of the corral.

But suspense is not a sustainable emotion, eventually people drifted away, not many but enough to make the thinning-out noticeable.

The battering and bawling continued. The gunsmith left, then several other men around the constable also departed. It was while Elrey and the priest were keeping the northward vigil, trying to assess each concerted charge of bulls against logs, the two men appeared from the south end of town.

There had been a third man but he had left the other two in order to rest his battered, tired body. That one was Jawn Kelly. The other two were Dodge Plummer's rangeboss Boss Cleaver and his tophand Chief Baca.

They were unwashed, rumpled, unshaven and sunken-eyed. When Elrey turned Boss Cleaver addressed the priest. 'You better pray that corral holds.'

Baca removed his hat, wiped off grime and sweat as he addressed Elrey. 'I think we got all of 'em. Someone had just worked cattle and turned them out. Boss thinks it was Jeffrey Mesa. Anyway, them bulls was around the cows like flies at a molasses bowl, and that helped. Otherwise we'd still be out there hunting.' Baca beat dust off with his hat before putting it back atop his head. Even in night-gloom he and Boss Cleaver looked exhausted. For several moments the small group listened as a particular hard charge against the corral's south logs made even the ground shake.

The little priest crossed himself again. This time the others noticed, and Boss Cleaver made a dry remark. 'I hope it works for you, Father, it never did for me.'

The cows, separate from the bulls but caught up by the furore bawled and also made light charges, but no one heeded that. It was the endless assaults of the big fighting bulls that people listened to.

Baca nodded and started to turn away. 'See you in the morning,' he said.

Elrey asked if he had seen a band of riders up north. Baca shook his head. He and his riders had met with good fortune. The freshly turned out cattle that had attracted the bulls had been something like six or eight miles from town.

At another time Boss and Chief would have asked questions; not tonight. They left Father Cross and the constable heading back down in the direction of the corral where they had left their horses. They would bed down in hay down there.

The racket north of town gradually diminished but it never stopped completely. The bulls exhausted themselves but their period of recovery was short. For the duration of the night they fought the corral, singly and in twos or threes, but the concerted wild charge of all the bulls at one time did not occur again for several hours.

Elrey went to his room leaving the little priest alone at the north end of town, working his beads and whispering supplications that the bulls would not break out of his strong but very battered corral, and since they did not break out, it seemed possible that his prayers were being answered, regardless of Boss Cleaver's scepticism about such things.

In the morning Boss Cleaver with the other Plummer riders left Coyanosa after an early breakfast, anxious to get back to the Plummer place.

Chief Baca told Boss Cleaver to let

Dodge Plummer know he would be along directly, and had an all-over bath at the shack for that purpose behind the tonsorial parlour, bought clean clothing and shocked hell out of the dour cafeman by eating two breakfasts and downing four cups of black java before he strolled over to the jailhouse where Elrey was idly thumbing dodgers someone had shoved under the jailhouse door yesterday probably late in the day, from the general store which was also the local postal facility.

Elrey pushed the dodgers aside and offered Baca coffee. Since he was already awash with the stuff he declined and eased down upon a bench as he said, 'There may be a few left out yonder, but if there are they'll be one hell of a distance off. Boss an' I decided when we found em' snortin' up those turned-out cows, we'd settle for what we saw.'

Chief gently wagged his head and smiled. 'You seen Jawn this morning?'

Elrey hadn't. 'No. Why?'

'He did good. Better'n some of the regular riders. But it was killin' him.' Baca's eyes twinkled. 'He'll sleep a week and use a quart of liniment before he feels human again.'

Elrey had counted the bulls. Twenty-seven. He had not expected more than perhaps fifteen. Evidently whoever had turned out those worked cows had done so to a lot of bulling critters.

Baca re-settled in the chair. Even his calloused saddle-parts were tender. 'Last night you asked if we'd seen a band of riders.'

'Renegades; they raided up north in the Guadalupe country. I guess it was pretty bad for some of the isolated outfits.'

Baca gazed thoughtfully at the constable for a long time before speaking again. 'I'm glad we didn't run into them. If we'd had to ride that far north . . . Elrey, you believe in a Protective Providence?'

Elrey sidestepped a direct answer as he replied. 'Last we heard is that the army is after them an' they fled west. But for a while it had folks scairt.'

Baca arose. He had another call to make before leaving town. At the door he asked if the holy father had a buyer for his bulls. To Elrey's knowledge he did not, but then he and the priest had not discussed this; there had been no point until, if and when, the bulls were corralled.

Because he did not want it to appear that he was following Chief Baca, Elrey let half an hour lapse before he too went down to Mex town.

Father Cross was in the old, softly aromatic chapel when Elrey found him. He turned back to one of the benches out back and waited.

When the priest emerged, he saw Elrey waiting, and with a little shrug said he had been giving thanks — and asking further that the corral would hold.

They exchanged a smile about that before Elrey asked if Father Cross had a buyer in mind for his cattle. The little priest made his fluttery hand gesture when he replied. 'No. How could I know the bulls would be here if I sent for a buyer?'

Elrey gravely regarded some of the straightened old grave markers beyond the edge of the tile-floored ramada. 'They can't be just left out there, Father. They got to have feed and water.'

'Do you think someone could drive a water wagon out there?'

Elery shrugged. There was no question that the corral strong enough to hold elephants had been weakened. 'Father, if they aren't fed and watered they'll shrink to beat hell.'

'Shrink?'

'Lose weight, get tucked-up-gaunt. A buyer will give you bottom dollar for critters with a bad weight loss. Anyway, they can't just be left out there this time of year without care.'

The little holy man sat with both hands in the fold of his robe. 'Can it be done, Elrey?'

'Father, it has to be done. Aside from the shrink, no stockman worth his salt would treat animals that way.'

' . . . Is Ramon Baca still in town? He could tell us about this.'

Elrey thought Chief probably was still in town, but after the rebuff he had received the last time he had visited Baca at the widow's house, he was reluctant to go over there again.

'He may be, Father. Even if he is he can't tell you anything I haven't said. Father, if you send someone to find a buyer today, and if one is found and starts for Coyanosa, it will be at the very least a couple of days, more likely a week before he gets here.' Elrey turned toward the priest. 'Livestock have to be cared for daily . . . Father, the next time you get an idea about raising money for the mission, will you talk it over with me first?'

The priest delayed his reply. He had already heard from two of the men who had built the corral, that it could not withstand the battering indefinitely, that no corral ever built could do that.

One thing was embedded in the holy father's mind: Never again as long as he lived, would he have anything to do with cattle, big razorback fighting cattle or the more docile redback cattle.

He finally spoke. 'Excuse me, Elrey, what did you say?'

The constable arose slowly. 'I'll see if the cattle can be watered.'

Father Cross watched the constable depart. He felt terrible for the trouble he had caused, not just to Elrey his friend, but to everyone else.

He hoisted the hem of his robe and ducked back into the chapel to kneel again at the altar. A long-suffering Son of God would surely understand, and yes, he would first discuss his next idea about raising money with Constable Austin.

The heat was coming. Lowing cattle, mostly complaining cows, were thirsty. The fighting bulls were too but their bellowing remained a fighting challenge.

Elrey saw Jawn Kelly sweeping the duckboards in front of his saloon and went up there. Jawn gazed stonily at him, offered no greeting and gimped his way back behind the bar to draw off two glasses of tepid beer. Not until he had half drained his glass did he speak.

Elrey, braced for a tirade, got a surprise. Jawn leaned on the bartop and smiled. 'Took me back over ten years. It was good to be with a bunch of riders again. I ache all over but that used to go with that line of work when I was younger — some of the time . . . I've known Chief and Boss Cleaver for years, but Elrey, you can know folks a long time an' think you know 'em. To really know 'em do somethin' like we did. That's where the boys is separated from the men.'

Elrey was caught off guard. He drank, put the glass down and regarded the saloonman before speaking. 'You fellers did a good job. The betting around town was about sixty-forty you'd never get it done.'

Jawn's smile widened. He took their glasses to the pump to be re-filled and returned with them. His gait was different, a little gimpy, but neither of them mentioned that.

As Jawn put the glasses down he said, 'While we was gone there was a scare about raiders?'

'Yeah. They wiped out some isolated ranches up north and fled west with the army behind them. What worried me was that you fellers might run into them. But Chief said you only went eight or ten miles up-country.'

Satisfied with the constable's reply, Jawn Kelly changed the subject. 'Father Cross got his buyer, has he?'

'No. He's goin' to send for one.'

Kelly's brows slowly lowered. 'It's hot out there. Them cattle need water.'

'And feed, Jawn. Even if his buyer shows up the next few days . . . '

'You goin' to haul water out there, Elrey?'

'Someone has to. Those cattle'll shrink to beat hell.'

Kelly downed his second beer and put the glass down hard. 'There's a water wago — .'

'It's already full and waiting for the horses to be hitched to it.'

Kelly dragged a limp sleeve across his lips before saying, 'Find Amos Sanchez. He knows longhorns damned near as well as Chief does. You'n Amos an' me can haul the water out there. I got a trough out back. It's old an' rusty but it don't leak.'

Elrey finished half the beer and shoved the glass away. 'You're already walkin' like you got a hot potato in your britches. I'll find Amos and someone else.'

Jawn Kelly straightened off the bar, blue eyes blazing. 'I don't need no one to tell me what I can an' can't do. Go find Amos an' meet me out back. Better yet, you'n him get a team on the wagon an' drive it up the alley behind the saloon. It'll take three of us to hoist the trough up.'

Elrey continued to lean against the

bar gazing at his friend. 'I worry about the corral holding. The minute those bulls see us coming they're going to raise hell.'

'It'll hold,' Kelly replied. 'We'll go slow an' make no fast moves. By now them critters will be too parched to bellow.' Because the constable still did not move Jawn Kelly's brows dropped again. 'We got to do it, Elrey. The corral will hold, but I don't like the idea of thirsty critters under a blazing sun. Go find Amos and get the wagon up behind the saloon.'

Elrey finally complied. Jawn Kelly locked his saloon for the second time and went to his rooms off the back of the building to apply liniment, get his hat and go out back to inspect the rusty old steel trough.

It held a lot of water. The trick was going to be to open the gate and drag the trough inside, then back the team, block the gate and fill the trough.

Elrey found Amos Sanchez taking a siesta beneath a shaggy old tree down in Mex town. He roused him and explained what had to be done. The tall older Mexican arose, scratched his head, took his hat down off a tree limb, mightily yawned and squinted skyward. The heat was already increasing. He excused himself, went inside the house, drank some bitter red wine and emerged looking as though he hadn't been napping.

As he and Elrey were walking toward the lower end of town to put a team on the water wagon, Amos said, 'You know, Jawn's tougher'n he looks. I wasn't used to that either, but either he's a good actor or he stood it better'n I did.' Amos smiled. 'I ate a horse last night, slept until sunrise, ate again and went to the hammock to sleep again when you came along. Jawn's a lot tougher than he looks.'

Elrey said nothing. Part of what Amos Sanchez had said was true: Jawn Kelly was a good actor.

They were harnessing a pair of greys to the water wagon when several local loafers drifted over to watch. One of them averred that if they were thinking of taking water out to those fighting bulls, the corral would finally give way. Another man, old and toothless, the colour of wet mud, added his grim prediction. 'Them bulls got blood in their eyes, they'll overrun the wagon, the team, and run you fellers down to make pulp-meat out of you.'

Amos smiled at the toothless Mexican and told him in Spanish he could drive; they would need another man. The toothless man walked briskly away and the others laughed.

Everyone the full length of the roadway who was outside saw the water wagon cross the main thoroughfare and turn north up the back alley in the direction of the saloon. People scattered to tell others. Before Amos, Elrey and Jawn Kelly had grunted the steel through onto the wagon, not only did all Coyanosa know what impended, but bets were again being placed. One man nearly had a heart seizure, the general store's proprietor. He ran out front yelling for someone to stop them; if the corral gave way the bulls would charge straight into town.

A lot of people heard him but only a few nervous ones thought he might be right, and neither these people nor the others, made a move to go behind the saloon.

9

The Unexpected

The lad who had climbed atop a roof the previous day with his father's telescope was back up there this morning, and this time his anxious mother said nothing. She was among the mostly silent, tense people lining the main thoroughfare as the water wagon appeared from the alleyway moving slowly toward the distant corral

Father Cross appeared out of a dog trot accompanied by the handsome widow named Bohorquez. She watched with a soft smile, the priest gripped his Crucifix in both hands.

The grey team had all they could handle with the load they were hitched to, and the ground was level. If there had been an incline they could not have done it.

Jawn Kelly was perched behind and above the team. His handling of the hitch made Elrey, who sat beside him, wonder how much handling of teams the saloonman had done.

The lanky man named Amos Sanchez probably shared Elrey's concern because while he clung to the metal bindings which secured the large wooden tank to the running gear, he watched Jawn rather than the corral or its occupants with their wicked long horns.

There probably had never been a wooden water tank that did not leak even after the swelling process had caused the kind of expansion which minimised leakage.

The people back in town appeared to be awaiting the violent reaction of the bulls as they watched the wagon moving ponderously forward.

Elrey was also watching ahead when he was satisfied the greys could keep the rig moving while at the same time behaving normally despite the unsure hands on the lines.

The bulling cows lowed but the big bulls lined the south side of the corral, hushed and still as they peered between massive log stringers.

Despite their other concerns, the smell of water kept them silent. They had been since the day before without it; quite possibly the majority of them had been much longer without it. It was the nature of bulls following the scent of bulling cows to ignore grazing or drinking for considerable periods of time in order to accomplish their basic function.

Elrey relaxed a little at a time. Jawn Kelly's concentration on what he was doing was total. He did not look ahead until it was time to begin lining out to the left in order to bring the heavy rig into the area of the corral gates, which faced west.

To Amos Sanchez, who had been a teamster, the problem was not getting out there or manoeuvring into place but backing the wagon to the gates.

Experienced teamsters often had trouble backing teams. Not every horse was wise enough to back a load. In fact not many horses learned to go backwards in a straight line; going backwards had to be learned, it was not normal to horses, especially backing in a straight line.

This was shortly to be put to the test.

The lad on the roof back in town had a bearing with his spyglass on something that held all his attention; a dust banner far to the west which appeared to be heading in the direction of Coyanosa. It was moving fast. The lad could not make out what was causing it, but instinct told him that whatever was coming, might reach the outskirts of town while the men with the water wagon were undertaking the most risky part of their venture, which was backing the rig to the gates, getting one of them open with the wagon against it, then blocking the gate while men wrestled the trough to the ground in a corral full of fighting bulls, and filling it with water.

He did not swing the spyglass toward the corral where Jawn Kelly's big semi-circular manoeuvre was making progress.

Amos Sanchez finally called to Jawn Kelly. 'You got one chance to be right. If you don't back the rig exactly to the gate, I don't think them bulls will wait for you to drive ahead and try again. They're thirsty enough to charge the gates if you have to pull out again.'

Jawn said nothing, but when he got to the end of his circling drive he eased the team out and around, squinted rearward to gauge the distance he had to back the rig, and let the lines lie slack for a few moments. This allowed the greys to prepare themselves for whatever came next. Fortunately they were older animals. Experienced at backing or not, they were experienced at what to them were the unpredictable, bizarre requirements made upon them by the two-legged critters who manned the lines, and waited now, ears back, for whatever was required of them.

Jawn was sweating but his expression was unrelenting. Maybe Amos was a better teamster, but Jawn had been the first to the high seat, had picked up the lines and since no one had suggested he might not be experienced at this sort of thing, he had driven.

Elrey sat twisted around so that he could tell Kelly which way to yaw the horses in case they did not know to back in a straight line. He thought the rig was aligned properly, but there was a considerable distance back to the gates. It would be up to Elrey to watch rearwards and it would be Jawn Kelly's responsibility to use his lines to keep the greys tracking backwards correctly, according to the directions Elrey called to him.

In town spectators were like statues, hushed, still and tense. One man's sniffing could be heard on both sides of the roadway. Another man, older and wearing a stained apron, spat amber, squinted and smiled without a shred of humour. The gunsmith had been a teamster.

The corralled animals, with the scent of water closer, milled fretfully but for the most part were quiet.

A rattling stagecoach came down from the north with its animals in an easy lope. Dust flew in its wake. As it came closer the driver and passengers saw what was occurring over west of the road at the big corral.

The whip hauled his horses down to trot. He and his passengers craned around for as long as they could.

Elrey wanted to swear. At this critical moment a distraction was certainly not needed.

Jawn eased his weight back on the lines, equal pressure on both leathers. The greys did not even hesitate. They'd had moments to relax and were now compatible. Also, not being young horses, and having been in harness hundreds of time, they understood what was being asked of them.

For about fifteen feet the water

wagon backed directly toward the gate, then one grey swung his rear until he was restrained by the tug, and got back into his proper place. The other grey horse put his head down and neither swerved nor hesitated. He knew what the backing manoeuvre was about.

Without looking around Jawn asked Elrey if they were properly aligned. They were. If Jawn held the horses to their present course the rear of the wagon would abut directly toward the middle of the southernmost gate. Elrey said, 'Perfect, hold them to it.'

The old gunsmith in town turned to a fair-complected man nearby whose eyes were obsidian to match his hair, and spoke in Spanish.

'Good. So far he is doing well.'

The Mexican made a droll reply in English. 'Why shouldn't he be? That's his business, getting something to drink to those in need.'

The lad on the house roof finally swung his spyglass toward the water wagon and the corral where large, very thirsty animals hardly moved as they watched the cause of that water-scent getting closer to their corral.

The lad swung his spyglass back in the direction of the oncoming dust cloud. He could see tiny figures out there but was unable to see anything well enough to make an identification.

He had thought at first it was cattle, perhaps being driven since cattle did not travel fast and were disinclined to move closely together. Later, he decided it was horsemen. What puzzled him was the idea that stockmen and their riders would not be running their horses just to get to town during the heat of the day.

He finally decided it was indeed horsemen, but not until they had appeared close enough for him to see sunlight reflecting off metal was he positive.

He was a long time coming to a frightening conclusion. Whoever they were, out there, there was a consider-able number of them and reflected light was not just off metal bits and spurs, it was also off saddlegun butt plates.

Working stockmen never carried saddleguns, at least they rarely did, and there were too many riders out yonder for them to belong to one ranch. It was more likely riders from several ranches together, or — and his hair stood up — or it was a large band of renegades. He had heard, along with everyone else in Coyanosa, about the troubles up north.

He was frightened, had to lower the spyglass to wipe sweat off before raising it again.

Elrey told Jawn to lean a little on the right line. When this was done the rear running gear of the water wagon ground slowly into a slewing movement until the rig was correctly aligned again.

Elrey said, 'Good. Just about perfect.'

Kelly's chin and nose dripped sweat, his shirt was dark with it. For the first time he spoke. 'What the hell is that — look toward town, Elrey. There's someone atop a house flapping his arms.'

Elrey turned, squinted, watched for a time then swore. 'Damed idiot.' Elrey twisted rearward again. The rig was less than a hundred feet from the corral, aligned perfectly.

The cattle were milling now, uneasy and bewildered. Along with two scents they were accustomed to, horse sweat and water, there was now a scent of men, and both by instinct and inclination, the longhorns had since calfhood associated the man smell with trouble.

Their milling did not necessarily presage a charge, but none of the men near the corral nor others watching from town, were confident that would not happen.

Jawn spoke from the side of his mouth. 'That damned idiot is flapping and yelling. Can you hear him?'

They were within about ten feet of one gate in perfect alignment. Elrey ignored the question to tell Amos Sanchez to climb down and get ready to open the gate.

The lanky man hit the ground lightly and walked very warily around the rig to the chain securing both gates. He worked with one eye on the bulls, who were watching him with heads lowered. Occasionally a bull would shake his head slightly, which was the age-old longhorn warning.

This was the crucial moment. In town watchers, including the priest and others from Mex town, were stone-still, scarcely breathing.

The lad on the rooftop was yelling and gesticulating. People turned indignantly looking for the source of that yelling. Only a few people could see the lad on the roof, but it was easier to hear him in town. What he was yelling was: 'Renegades! Big band of renegades comin' from out yonder!'

People who heard but did not see him, acted stunned for moments. Others, like the old gunsmith, did not need time to adjust to this fresh peril, they ran for weapons and cried out for others to do the same.

Out at the corral Amos Sanchez moved swiftly from the gate to the front of the wagon and pointed as he called up to Jawn Kelly and the constable. 'That kid on the roof — he's yelling about renegades. There's dust . . . '

Elrey sat forward, tipped down his hat and Jawn Kelly slackened the pressure on the lines, shook off sweat, sat for a long moment squinting in the direction of the rising dust, then swore as he moved to climb down. Elrey caught his arm. 'Get those horses moving! Get back to town!'

It was too far to run on foot. Jawn Kelly fumbled for the lines and yelled at the greys. They leaned into their collars as Jawn snapped their rumps with the leathers.

Excitement was readily transferred from men to animals. The greys heaved into a lumbering trot with the cumbersome water wagon gathering momentum. Jawn made a big half circle, anything sharper would have upset the wagon. He got the greys lined out.

In town people were running and yelling to each other. The lad on the roof was standing upright with the spyglass to his face. He abruptly lowered the glass and climbed down off the roof.

The bulls, as well as the less unpredictable cows, aggravated by the abrupt lessening of the scent of water, bawled and milled, fought their restraining logs and raised dust.

Elrey left the wagon before it stopped moving. Amos Sanchez did the same. By the time Jawn Kelly got the momentum of all that weight down to manageable condition, he and the rig were almost at the lower end of the town on the west side. Jawn was the last one to jump down and run back, abandoning the wagon and its horses. The greys were content to stand, at least until they caught their wind.

Men yelling back and forth, rushing

for positions of vantage, raising road-way dust, were in contrast to the man who owned the general store. He and his clerk were closing the steel shutters out front. A barrel of apples was left in place out front, along with several swatches of dress material looped over a round rod.

Jawn Kelly was breathless when he reached his saloon, hastened on through to his living quarters and fumbled nervously with his shellbelt and holstered Colt. The last thing he grabbed was a saddlegun with no bluing left on it.

Elrey yelled at passing townsmen without arms to hand out weapons from his wall rack.

Somewhere at the upper end of Coyanosa someone was making a racket beating a triangular piece of steel, the kind ordinarily employed at cow outfits to announce mealtime.

Down at the blacksmith's shop the smith and his helper were leaning calmly in their doorway watching all the frantic activity. Each was armed with a rifle, each man had a sidearm buckled around his waist.

Watchers at the back of town yelled warning as the hard-riding marauders came closer. There was no gunfire, which was probably unusual with all the excited people with guns in hand, but if there had been it would have served no good purpose, the small army of renegades was still beyond gun range.

But not for long.

Elrey went around into the alley behind his horse shed. The heat haze which would eventually impair visibility was not yet in place. It was possible to see the oncoming, heavily-armed raiders quite clearly while they were still a fair distance from town.

Elrey turned as someone came from behind. It was Pat Cullough from the way-station. He had a rifle instead of a carbine. Without a word he moved ahead of Elrey to lean his gun barrel across a corral stringer and take very careful aim.

Elrey said, 'Too far, Pat.'

The way-station boss squeezed off the first shot. He and Elrey waited for the result. There was none. Evidently the oncoming renegades did not hear the gun and since none of their horses shied, it was probable that what Elrey had said was true; the distance was too great even for a rifle.

Cullough opened the breech of his rifle, ejected the spent casing and methodically inserted a fresh cartridge and leaned down again, snugging the butt back tightly, taking his time aiming, then fired again.

This time two horses shied. Cullough hit nothing but the renegades knew they were now under attack. They carried carbines which lacked the range of Cullough's rifle, nevertheless they returned the fire, smoke enveloped them briefly as they came on, and somewhere there was a sound of shattering glass.

Elrey left the way-station boss back

there and hastened around front to the roadway. There were only two people in sight, the storekeeper and his helper struggling to force a stubborn steel shutter closed.

Elrey guessed Coyanosa's vigilance committeemen were in place, mostly on the west side of town which was the direction the renegades were coming from.

He returned to the alley where Pat Cullough had got off another long-range shot. This time, too, he made a horse shy from a near-miss, but none of the wild-charging horsemen left his saddle.

Whoever had been beating that triangle stopped doing it. Not a single dog barked; town dogs were especially attuned to the moods of their owners. Panic or near panic was always transmittable. The dogs were silent because they had gone into hiding, either in their houses or under porches, somewhere anyway that they sought safety.

10

Chaos!

A rattle of gunfire accompanied by gouts of dirty smoke blossomed in an uneven, staggered way from the west side of town.

Hard-riding horsemen make poor targets. It seemed to Elrey that most of the gunshots were too high, over the heads of the raiders, whom he could see very well by now.

The Mexicans among them wore traditional bandoleers crossed over their upper bodies. The other raiders had nothing that distinctive. They were weathered-dark men, unshorn and unshaven, slovenly and dirty, individuals without redeeming virtues, human scavengers and murderers of the worst kind.

A number of reasons had been put

forth over the years about these bands; some claimed they were amoral dregs left over after the Civil War. Others held that they were organised bands of rustlers and horsethieves who had banded together to attack isolated ranches and villages. Whatever their reason for existing, no one disputed their savagery. They used torture as indiscriminately as they used murder, they made no distinction when they shot people, and the stronger their groups became the more ferocious and overwhelming their attacks were.

There was no worse scourge than renegade bands. The army had been run ragged chasing them. They knew every trick and tactic, and while they commonly came with a setting sun behind them, or a rising sun in front, their notoriety made people dread them more than Apaches or Comanches.

Elrey watched and wondered briefly about a raid in broad daylight before sundown. Intuition told him it was probably about equal parts fury over being pursued up north by soldiers, and whiskey.

He was right, but with gunfire and acrid smoke making calm thought impossible, he joined several men including the way-station boss and others trying to empty saddles as the renegades raced ahead.

When the firing from both sides clouded the air the renegades made a surprising manoeuvre, they veered abruptly southward toward the lower end of town. Their reason could have been for different notions among their leaders, but it at least accomplished confusion, which meant reduced gunfire from the defenders of Coyanosa.

Men watched, then hurried in different directions to attempt a defence in a different direction, but the renegades swept across the lower end of town before more than a few defenders got that far south to use their weapons.

Elrey joined others in sprinting to the other side of the roadway. There was an alley on the east side of town, beyond which was Mex town. Because all but a few of the buildings on that side of town had been built close together, the defenders had to crowd close to the few intervening dog trots. There was little gunfire during this period until the raiders charged into Mex town, then their gunfire erupted en masse. A few Mexicans, who had not been close to their residences were killed, others were wounded, screams arose among the adobe structures. A few armed Mexicans tried to pick off men whirling and charging on wild-eyed mounts. If there were any accurate shots there was no sign of it among the devil's horsemen as they reined left and right, firing, raising dust and spreading gunsmoke. The noise was deafening. People huddled behind barred doors holding their children flat to earthen floors.

Spent brass cartridge casings glistened in the dust. The time required for the renegades to pause long enough to reload was taken up by their comrades whose guns were not shot out.

The door of the Mex town cantina was shot off its hinges. If there had been glass windows they too would have been destroyed. Bullets could not penetrate mud walls three feet thick otherwise the number of dead and wounded would have been much higher.

Before enough defenders from the west side of town could deploy in the alley on the east side, the renegades had completely cowed Mex town and were milling, shouting to one another about pushing ahead into the main part of Coyanosa.

Defenders got off several ragged volleys, but the alley was an unprotected place. The renegades fired back killing several men including the blacksmith's helper and the man who occasionally helped Jawn Kelly at his saloon.

The others scattered seeking cover as the renegades swung their mounts to charge northward in the direction of the upper end of town.

Elrey watched, guessed their purpose, leathered his gun and ran harder than he had run in his life. What aided him immeasurably was a rattle of gunfire from several of the northerly *jacals* where terrified but infuriated women leaned rifles and carbines past deeply recessed *jacal* windows and fired a withering blast.

Finally, two saddles were emptied in the plaza. Renegades reacted to this fresh defiance by howling like Comanches as they reined desperately toward shelter, around beside buildings, behind buildings and even in some cases forced their mindless mounts inside structures with wide enough openings, and one man was shot point-blank as he crashed through a doorway by an old man whose rifle was a genuine antique.

Their leader rallied them and led a rush northward past the *jacals* where renegades fired through widows where women with guns had been. The noise was deafening.

Elrey's heart was trying to break out of his chest, his legs pumped at maximum capacity. He lost his hat as he ran and nearly lost his sixgun because the tie-down was not in place, but he put his palm on the butt and held it there for the last thirty yards of his rush.

He felt no heat and heard none of the bedlam back in town. By the time he reached the priest's log corral the renegades were emerging from Mex town and swinging to their left to charge down the main roadway where Coyanosa's stores were.

Elrey had sweat stinging his eyes as he fumbled with the chain of the corral. The longhorns inside were in a frenzy because of the gunfire and panic southward in town. They were also maddened by thirst.

He got the gates open, got behind one gate as the wild bulls charged clear. He fired three times to turn them toward town. They veered southward, twenty-seven big longhorn fighting bulls with their blood up.

Ahead were horsemen, noise and gunsmoke. Ahead too was the scent of water.

The bulls charged the town. They swept southward in a ragged line, heads high, eyes glassy, powerful bodies moving with saddle-horse speed.

The renegades were swinging southward down the main roadway. Their backs were to the oncoming bulls as they shot out windows, riddled store fronts and yelled their challenges.

The old gunsmith fired through a partially opened door. Four renegades whirled and raced past firing into the door. Southward at Jawn Kelly's saloon, a shotgun blast from both barrels downed a horse and mangled the left leg of its rider. The man was pinned. His screams rose above the other sounds. Several of his companions paused long enough to look back — and got the fright of their lives.

Red-eyed longhorn bulls were entering town in a dead run. The renegades fired at them then whirled and raced ahead toward the lower end of town unmindful of their comrades or the firing of townsmen.

Some of the raiders saw the solid front of enraged wild bulls with shiny long horns coming at them and tried to warn the others with screams. The bulls charged into the rearmost of the raiders heads down and eyes closed. Two horses were lifted four feet into the air and slammed against store fronts. They went through the wood as though it were paper and lay dead inside the buildings.

Upright posts which held overhangs in front of most buildings along the main roadway were knocked loose. The wounded renegade pinned beneath his dead horse disappeared beneath the hooves of raging bulls. After they swept past his dead horse was still recognisable but the man was not.

The renegades, on exhausted horses, left off firing and concentrated on trying to get out of Coyanosa at the southern end.

The bulls were thirsty but far from exhausted. They overtook mounted renegades, upset their horses and in several cases when frantic renegades abandoned horses and tried to run toward hiding places among the buildings, they were skewered from behind and flung off like broken dolls.

The way-station boss was at the lower end of town with his rifle. He shot from inside an old roofless *jacal* which had one recessed window opening facing the roadway. He shot the first fleeing renegades.

The main roadway looked like a battlefield. There were nine dead bulls, several dead horses and at least six dead renegades.

Elrey returned to town at a slower gait than he had used leaving it half an hour earlier. By the time he got back the renegades were racing past the southernmost building, their number considerably reduced.

They were no longer firing weapons,

they were trying to out-distance long-horn bulls to whose earlier agitation had been added the scent of blood, and they were losing the race because they had already ridden their mounts to the point of collapse.

One horse abruptly folded his knees and fell. His rider in a fit of rage shot the horse in the head, which was actually a kindness, the horse was wind-broken.

But the enraged renegade had wasted one precious moment. The nearest bull probably would have caught him anyway, but now as he turned to flee a mottled longhorn whose mouth was open, tongue lolling, veered to one side, dropped his head and swept it upwards. The renegade's scream could be heard back up through town.

Elrey caught several townsmen as they emerged from shelter to watch the chase below town, told them to round up anyone they found and join him in the alley on the west side of town with their guns and horses.

He was sweaty, dusty, his legs ached and his heart was still racing as he went around behind the jailhouse to rig out the freshly-shod horse, a big, roman-nosed sorrel as tough as rawhide.

He moved slowly, mindful of the noise beyond town where fleeing renegades and stumbling horses tried to veer clear of their comrades in a hope that the bulls would not follow, but there were still enough bulls to pursue each renegade. The number of raiders was down to about a dozen, it would have been impossible to count either the fleeing horsemen or the bulls getting in among them. There was a cloud of dust twenty feet high and almost thick enough to chew.

Elrey led nine townsmen southward from Coyanosa riding in a slow lope. He did not want to get close enough to divert the bulls, who were doing a good job without assistance.

Back in town the priest helped the wounded, among them the rugged old gunsmith. The road was a broad expanse with broken store fronts, dangerously tilted overhangs and debris including dead animals and men, its full length. There were surprisingly few wounded except down in Mex town where two of the female snipers had been shot dead, four others had been wounded, and four men caught by surprise in the plaza had been shot dead.

The wounded and injured received the best care possible in a town that had only an elderly midwife and a priest to care for them.

Southward with the sun high and hot, and with no shade for miles, exhausted horses stumbled, some gave out completely and others went through the motions of running, but were actually doing nothing more than rising up and coming down without covering much ground.

The renegades sat sideways shooting at the bulls, who seemed impervious as they finally overtook the fleeing outlaws and lunged to the attack.

From back where Elrey and his armed townsmen watched, one man said, 'Gawddamn. I never even dreamt of such a thing.'

Four renegades abandoned failing horses and huddled behind two dead bulls, one shot ahead of the other, which fell atop the first one. It was the only safe place as the pursuit whirled past. One of the desperate outlaws stood up with his carbine and shot a bull from behind. Pat Cullough left the saddle, raised his rifle and caught the renegade before he could get back down.

The man fell among his companions, who unceremoniously rolled him away and watched the constable and his riders approach.

They were breathless, thoroughly demoralised and covered with sweaty dust. One of them told the others not to fire on the riders, which was the prudent thing to do, although if they could have known what was to come, they might have fought to the death.

A man caught afoot by a wild bull fell to the ground as the big animal dropped his head. He was caught by both horns and did not cry out as others had done as he was flung high to fall limply ten feet away. More fortunate than others who were gored, he had died almost instantly when both horns plunged through him.

Elrey dropped down to a walk. Six bulls were still in pursuit of three mounted renegades. The terrified riders twisted to fire back. They had to empty their guns to accomplish it, but they killed three of the bulls. After that, guns empty, they flung forward to ride hard, but their horses were sucking air like bellows and had nothing left to give as the remaining bulls overtook them. All three renegades leant to the ground where they could aim better than on the back of a horse. The bulls were among them in moments. One man screamed, another shot the bull at the moment the bull gored him. The third man snapped his empty gun twice, hurled it at the nearest bull and ran as hard as he could — in a straight line. He was knocked down by one bull and charged over by the next one. It took him a while to die with a crushed skull and a broken back he could not have survived as the bull that had first charged him came around, head near the ground, to make a goring run. One huge horn burrowed below the man, who was limp enough to roll off otherwise he would have been hurled into the air.

Elrey stopped within gun range of the forted up renegades. He and his companions watched the end of the bloody pursuit. The only outlaws still alive were three men behind the piled-up bulls. One of them raised a carbine with a filthy rag tied to the end of it.

Elrey called to him. 'Pitch the guns out where we can see them. Boot knives, derringers, anything you got.'

Guns sailed over the dead bulls, two knives followed. Elrey said, 'Stand up!'

'No by gawd,' a renegade called stoutly back.

Elrey smiled coldly. 'Mister, if we wanted to shoot you, all we'd have to do is ride down there and do it. You pitched your guns away. *Stand up!*'

They arose slowly, filthy, bedraggled men with vicious faces and cold, deadly eyes. There was not a really young man among them; they looked to be either in their forties or fifties, but perhaps years of dissipation and hard-living had made them look old.

'Walk out from behind the bulls,' Elrey told them.

They obeyed. One man, shorter than the others, thickly built and obviously strong as an ox, spat cotton, pushed sweat and dust off his lined, leathery face and said, 'That feller with the long blond hair that got shot as we was leavin' town — he was the head In'ian. Burke Devlin. Maybe you heard of him. He's got dodgers on him from Montana to Messico. Plenty of reward money, mister.'

Elrey gestured with his thumb. 'Start walking, you sons of bitches. Head back to town. I said — *walk!*' They walked. Elrey and his riders watched them go over to the road and turn north, they dragged their feet and slumped as they walked. Once, a man turned to speak and Elrey leveled a finger at him. 'There's not a gawddamned word I want to hear out of you. Face forward an' keep walking.'

It was hot. Already dead animals and men were beginning to swell. Up in town they watched the riders returning driving three survivors in front. Not much was said but there were a lot of bitter thoughts. Every dead resident of Coyanosa had been someone's friend.

11

The Ride Out and the Ride Back

It required two days to haul dead animals away and prepare the dead for burial. In Mex town funerals were ordinarily noisy affairs. This time because of the wanton murders hearts were sad, silent and fiercely bitter.

Father Cross prayed over the dead on both sides of town, and this time when the town carpenter was busiest rebuilding store fronts and ruined overhangs, he took time to recommend that the Coyanosa town council erect a monument to the dead, and received the job of carving such a thing.

It was almost a month before he got around to it, but when he did he worked for two days and when the monument to the Great Raid Of 1881 was finished he had done something which to that time had not been done, he sprinkled the names of the dead in Mex town among the dead in the predominantly gringo section of Coyanosa indiscriminately.

When he was questioned about this by the sniffing proprietor of the general store he simply said, 'Blood is red regardless of whatever is different. Folks from different parts of town fought a common enemy in defence of a town that belongs to all of us. But if the council don't like my sign . . . '

The few objections never surfaced again.

There was almost a full week of burials and mourning, of unsmiling faces and a growing swell of cold and deadly feeling about Elrey's prisoners. At the beginning an outraged cafeman refused to supply food for them. He came around only when Elrey threatened to arrest him and toss him in the same cell with the renegades.

But as days passed the resentment increased. Everyone had known the dead. The last person to die was the old gunsmith. Elrey was at his bedside with the priest and the dowdy midwife when he was dying. His passing marked the last death resulting from the raid. He left this vale of sweat and tears on the fourth day. Before passing he beckoned for Elrey to lean close as he said, 'I'm ready, partner. Last year or so my eyes been failin' an' my legs get weak if I stand too long. Them's signs of a carcass wearin' out. I never wanted to hang on past a useful time.'

He didn't; he died about an hour after saying that to Elrey.

The reaction through town was stony, dead silence. The number of dead had climbed steadily. Each death was another contributing factor to the smouldering fury in survivors' hearts.

As long as men were occupied hauling dead animals away, helping the town carpenter and digging graves, the bitter, cold fury was dormant. It was there, it did not atrophy, but other things — the business of the living — kept them busy.

On the fifth day old Dodge Plummer rode in with his crew. They were solemn as they tied up out front of the jailhouse.

Dodge's men ambled up to Kelly's place as Dodge entered Elrey's office and sank into a chair. He looked worn and tired. Without a preliminary he said, 'Them bastards caught Jeff Mesa in the yard of an evening with his riders.' Dodge fell to examining broken, dirty fingernails. 'We seen buzzards and rode over there day afore yestiddy . . . Took us two days to get all the dead buried. Looks to me like them renegades rode up about sundown and began shooting. We examined some weapons. Jeff's pistol hadn't been fired at all. Other guns had one shot-out casing, or maybe two — They sure as hell wasn't expecting it. Them renegades left a lot of ejected casings around the west side near the barn an' bunkhouse. From that we figure they snuck up in the dusk . . . They even shot Jeff's dog . . . Looks like the town took a shellacking too.'

Elrey re-told the story without haste. When he was finished old Dodge Plummer's perpetually narrowed eyes rested on him. 'You got three prisoners?'

'Yeah.'

'Why didn't you kill the sons of bitches when you caught 'em?'

Elrey leaned forward on his desktop. 'They give up, threw their weapons away.'

Dodge continued to regard Elrey from steely eyes. He sighed and wagged his head. 'Elrey, in my time if we caught 'em like that, we shot 'em where they stood, or hanged 'em, dependin' on whether there was trees handy or not . . . What're you goin' to do with them?'

'Hold them until a circuit judge comes to town.'

'An when'll that be? Them fellers ride through a lot of towns, they hold a lot of trials. One may not show up in Coyanosa for a hell of a spell.'

'Then I'll keep holding them,' Elrey said.

The old man arose, considered his toilworn hands then said, 'How many them bulls left?'

'As far as I know, none are left. We been haulin' their carcasses miles away for days. I didn't make a count but we had twenty-seven corralled.'

'I know. Chief and Boss told me.'

'Well, I saw seven dead in the roadway when I left town to run down the last of the renegades, and I think there was another thirteen or fourteen dead along the south stageroad.'

Dodge tallied that and looked troubled. 'There're still some around, then.'

Elrey shrugged. He did not know whether there were or not. From what he had seen the slaughter of fighting bulls had been especially decimating. They had pursued renegades for several miles close enough to attack them, and they had been shot at during the entire chase.

Dodge made a surprising remark. 'By my calculation they was worth four, five dollars a head for meat. Well, if they're plumbed wiped out, why then seems to me folks here in town owe them for savin' Coyanosa.'

Dodge went to the door but did not open it. He spoke again in a thoughtful way. 'An' us stockmen — don't matter how it was done, but the bulls was taken off our range . . . I'd be willin' to ride around hat in hand.' Dodge made a sorry small smile. 'I'll sweeten the pot by pitchin' in the first fifty dollars.'

After Plummer left Elrey sat a moment at his desk thinking of the successful, bloody strike against Jeff Mesa, an individual he had never liked very much, but a man who certainly did not deserve to be massacred along with his riders — and their dog.

He was about to leave the office when Jawn Kelly walked in, freshly shaved and smelling of the French toilet water the Coyanosa barber liberally sprinkled his patrons with.

189

Jawn's some-time helper had been among the killed. Ordinarily a blunt man, Kelly mentioned the deed, the devastation, and finally said he had heard across his bar there was a surviving renegade holed up east of town at a place called Oak Canyon.

Elrey's brows climbed a little. This was the first he had heard of a fourth surviving renegade. Jawn shrugged, his eyes on the rack of guns against the far wall. 'We made up a tally at the saloon last night, before I heard that story. We come up with twenty dead renegades. That's how many been buried by coffin count. How many was there? The most figure I hear was twenty four or five.' Jawn Kelly put his startlingly blue gaze on the constable. 'You got three locked up. That leaves two. There's one holed up in Oak Canyon, that leaves one — unless there's two holed up over there.'

Jawn looked Elrey squarely in the eye. 'I got no idea whether he — they — got horses or not. Maybe one of 'em's hurt, but I can tell you for a fact that when the feller was tellin' me that story there was a dozen listeners along the bar.'

Elrey had no trouble with the implication. As he arose he said, 'You want to ride along?'

Jawn left his chair and shook his head. 'I'm still recuperating from my last horseback trip.'

Elrey crossed over where Dodge Plummer and his men were mounting. He told Dodge what Jawn had said and asked if the old cowman wanted to ride along.

Dodge slowly wagged his head while looking down from the saddle. 'We're behind at home. Spent a lot of time buryin' Jeff and his men.' Dodge lifted his rein hand. 'Be careful out there,' he said, nodded and turned toward the centre of the roadway with his silent riders following.

Elrey buckled a carbine boot under the fender of his saddle, led the roman-nosed sorrel out of the corral and rode up the back alley until he could see the priest's battered corral, then cut on a diagonal course across the stage road heading for the oak-studded, grassy secluded canyon — actually little more than a wide and deep arroyo — named after the variety of ancient trees that grew down in its depths.

What made this ironic was that Oak Canyon was within the boundary of Jeffrey Mesa's deeded range.

He did not hasten. Whoever was holed up there, providing he was still there, had to have a horse; Oak Canyon was many miles northeast of where the last of the renegades had been captured. If he was wounded and desperate enough, he undoubtedly had the weapons to defy the constable with.

Elrey had heard several tallies of dead bulls and dead outlaws. They varied as much as six to eight by head counts. He rode along wondering if there would ever be a truly accurate count. He believed at least one or two of the bulls had survived. And despite a generally accepted figure in the high twenties for the raiders, he never once on his ride toward Oak Canyon, suspected that all the renegades had been accounted for.

In fact for years after the raid, stories continually surfaced of surviving outlaws. That too was not unusual. Both Jesse James and Billy Bonney were alive and well, Billy on a ranch in Mexico, Jesse with his brother out in California.

For whatever reason, people did not want to relinquish either their heroes or their villains. With the passage of time legends assumed a life of their own.

Elrey thought he might be riding toward one now as he caught his first sight of black and white oaks above the place called Oak Canyon.

His mistake was not to sashay back and forth looking for tracks. It did not occur to him. If there was a renegade hiding in the canyon he would know about it soon enough.

There was no fugitive in Oak Canyon

and never had been.

Elrey used up a solid hour after tethering his horse back from the edge of the canyon in oak shade while he took the carbine and walked ahead.

There was heat but a mitigating circumstance was a high veil in front of the sun which appeared to reach from horizon to horizon.

There was no wind, not even a breeze, the air was still and slightly heavy, as though perhaps a storm was on the way.

Elrey was only conscious of his stalk to the edge of the canyon. What made this easy was the scattering of old trees that grew right up to the west verge of the canyon.

He got up there and hunkered with his Winchester leaning aside to block in squares of the area below while he searched each square for signs of a man, or maybe two men.

He abandoned that after finding nothing, on the grounds that they could be down there doing exactly as Elrey was doing, sitting motionless in oak shade.

He searched for horses without ever finding any. He knew the trails down from the rims but hesitated about using them to get down there because they were exposed from the heights to the canyon floor.

He finally got back away from the edge and hiked northward. There was a rock slide up there with boulders large enough to conceal a man descending from above.

Rock slides were notoriously unstable footing. Unless he was extremely careful descending he would make enough noise to be heard.

When he got up there the sun was on its westerly slide. Elrey squatted a moment beside an oak tree, leaned on his Winchester while studying the southward run of the canyon.

By the time he was prepared to attempt the descent the sun had descended another notch or two.

It required skill and patience to move

slowly from boulder to boulder during the descent without starting a noisy little rock slide.

By the time he reached flat ground the sun had slipped down a little farther; there were shadows forming along the barranca walls where daylight no longer reached.

Visibility down here was nowhere nearly as good as it had been up above. For one thing oak trees were thick, for another thing, despite clear sign of deer browsing off tall underbrush, the flourishing growth was still in places taller than Elrey.

He began his stalk southward.

Not until he was mid-way into the canyon did he begin to wonder. There were no hoof imprints, no droppings, no sign of grass having been cropped.

He pushed farther southward until he could look up and see the verge where he first spied downward.

He moved with less caution from this point on until he reached the best and widest trail from above. Over there he stood a long while considering trail-dust which showed every scurrying mouse track, every four-toed sign of quail and other birds crossing, and no sign of either boots tracks or horseshoe imprints.

He went over beside a massive but not very tall black oak and leaned. Not only was no one down here, but from the sign, there had not been, at least not since summer dust had settled.

He did not retrace his steps to get out of the canyon, he walked boldly up the dusty trail in plain sight of anyone who could have been in the canyon.

By the time he got back to his horse he was breathing hard. The sorrel had dozed the full time his rider had been gone. Horse-like, he jerked awake at the sound of boots.

Elrey turned back the way he had come without hurrying. He had several misgivings about what had happened. The uppermost one was that he had been sent on this wild goose chase for a very valid reason which he chose not to dwell upon.

Dusk settled before he was half way back to Coyanosa. That high veil which had prevented the day from becoming uncomfortably hot was still in place. Stars shone, but in a misty, watery manner.

He could see town lights miles before he arrived in Coyanosa. When he reached the north-south stage road he could have boosted the sorrel into a lope. Instead he plodded along at a dead walk on a loose rein.

A massive old high-sided freight wagon being pulled along by twelve mules was snail-pacing its way toward town, every creak and groan audible for a considerable distance.

Elrey passed it still riding at a walk, exchanged a wave with the freighter and his swamper without saying a word.

After he had passed the freighter, a burly, unwashed and unshorn man, spat over the side, squinted ahead and told his swamper who the rider had been.

He also told him Elrey Austin had never before failed to call a greeting when they met.

The swamper, a lean man much younger than the freighter, made a casual remark. 'Maybe in the dark you was mistaken, Mike.'

The freighter, sitting hunched with slack lines in his hands shook his head. 'I ain't mistaken, Orry. I've been to Coyanosa a hunert time since I been hauling. Something's bothering him.'

The closer Elrey got to town the more solid his misgiving became. Everything up ahead looked normal, town lights, faint sounds of men and equipment, the calls of mothers to their children to come inside, it was nigh bedtime.

He was abreast of Father Cross's battered bull corral and scarcely glanced at it the first time and would not have glanced at it the second time if his horse hadn't raised its head, snorted and shied slightly.

Elrey turned the horse facing the

corral, stopped and sat there for a long time before urging the reluctant animal to leave the road and approach the corral.

The roman-nosed sorrel had to be forced. Whatever scent had frightened him still did until he finally balked about a hundred feet away and could not be made to go closer.

12

Aftermath

That high mist which partially obscured stars and a belated moon made the old battered, empty corral ghost-like even close up. Both massive gate posts had been forced to lean after repeated assaults on them by lunging bulls.

The cross-member about ten or twelve feet above the ground which held the posts together at the top had three dangling bodies suspended from it.

There was not a sound, no movement, just the eerie, obscure light from above which was sufficiently veil-like to make details difficult to discern even at close range.

A foraging owl swept low on silent wings, did not see the man and horse until the last minute, then beat frantically with powerful wings to get clear.

That was the only sound, a whisper-like beating of strong wings.

The sorrel horse was uncomfortable and motionless, attuned to the slightest movement of the man on his back.

Elrey placed both hands atop the saddlehorn and sat a long time before dismounting with one split-rein in his hand. The horse followed the man on foot where he would not have taken the man on his back, but he ducked his head often and made a faint sound from distended nostrils.

Elrey stood below looking up. He had been sure who they were even from a considerable distance, and he was correct: His three renegade prisoners from the jailhouse. They had been dead long enough for their facial expressions to be smoothed out after their initial terror. They did not particularly look at peace, they simply looked dead.

Elrey turned his back and leaned on the corral gazing in the direction of town. *Jawn Kelly*.

Despite their long acquaintanceship he had been part of the conspiracy; if it hadn't been for Kelly's convincing story of a renegade or two out at Oak Canyon Elrey would not have left town.

Some men would have been grateful. Elrey Austin was not. He mounted tiredly and walked the sorrel down to the back alley behind his jailhouse, put the horse up, pitched feed, made sure the trough was full, then entered the *juzgado* from out back.

He did not light the lamp but stood behind one of the front windows looking in the direction of Kelly's saloon, from which faint noises were audible even at that distance.

He felt bitter; they were up there celebrating, probably laughing at having hoodwinked the constable.

The cell room door was open. He went down, recognised the signs of a fierce struggle, saw his copper circlet with the cellroom keys on it, picked it up and returned to the office to replace it upon the wall-nail behind his desk. He examined the roadway door which he had not locked before going to Oak Canyon, found no signs of forcing although when the door was closed from the outside, the little metal strip on the inside fell into a hanger, and could only be raised from the outside by considerable pressure.

He cracked the door and ran his fingers down the inside edge of the door and the outside edge of the jamb. Someone had inserted a knife, got it beneath the inside latch, and had lifted. The door would then swing inward without a sound.

He put up his booted carbine, washed his face and hands out back, then sat at his desk for an hour, or until Coyanosa retired. He then went over to the east-side alley, went up as far as Jawn Kelly's back door, which was massive and kept closed by a thick *tranca* on the inside. When the *tranca* was in place the door could not be opened from the outside.

He struck the door several times with the barrel of his beltgun. When there was no response he struck it three times much harder.

This time he heard swearing and heavy movement inside the building, put up his weapon and was leaning in semi-darkness when a water-eyed, tousled-headed saloonman opened the door prepared to snarl. Elrey did not say a word, he put his palm against the saloonman's chest and pushed.

Inside, it was dark. Jawn turned on bare feet and without a word padded to his living quarters, lighted a hanging lamp, went to sit on the side of his rumpled bed and shook his head. 'I had nothin' to do with it, Elrey.'

The constable let himself wearily down into a chair. 'Jawn, you sent me on that wild goose chase.'

Kelly's brow furrowed. 'I told you; a feller at the bar told me there was one holed up out there.'

'What feller?'

Jawn ran a hand through his awry

hair as he replied. 'A rangeman. I don't know his name but I've seen him in town a few times. I think he rides for Dodge Plummer. Skinny feller with a prominent adam's apple.'

Elrey shifted in the chair. 'How did he know?'

'Hell Elrey, I got no idea. Like I told you, there was talk. You know how fellers gang up on an idea along the bar. An' partner, let me tell you for a fact, most folks in town was in favour of lynching those bastards.'

'Which men from town took them up there?'

This time Kelly's protestation of innocence was accompanied by a gesture with both hands. 'Elrey, as Gawd's my witness, I was busy last night. Lots of fellers was in. First I knew anything was when a couple fellers went out, and come rushin' back after a while white in the face. They yelled that someone had taken your prisoners out of the jailhouse and hung 'em from the cross member at the

206

priest's corral north of town. That's the gospel truth.

'Some of us went out into the roadway, but we had to walk up north a ways before we could make them out swingin' by the neck out there.' Jawn Kelly's intensity increased, he leaned forward, hands clasped.

'If some fellers in town done it, I don't know who they were. Last night I had a lot of trade. I could name off who was in the saloon if you want me to. I think I can remember most of 'em.'

Elrey let his gaze wander around the poorly lighted room with its spartan furnishings before he eventually spoke again.

'I'm goin' to find them, Jawn.'

Elrey arose, they looked steadily at each other for a long moment before Jawn said, 'Elrey; it's done. They're dead and you'll have a hell of a time gettin' anyone to say they didn't deserve lynching.' Jawn stood up in his nightshirt. 'Maybe you'll find something out. My guess is that no one's goin' to tell you a damned thing. Not because they helped lean on the ropes but because the whole town was in favour of what happened, an' folks aren't goin' to see whoever done it get into trouble . . . Elrey, just let it drop. It's over an' done with, isn't it?'

After Elrey departed the same way he had entered, by the alleyway, Jawn Kelly did not immediately return to his bed, he padded through to his bar, had a stiff drink leaning on the counter in quiet gloom, and let go a long sigh.

Elrey was going to make himself unpopular by pushing things. Coyanosa was a long way from cities where the law prevailed according to written edict. For a lot longer than any living residents of Coyanosa could remember, the law in New Mexico's southerly regions had been interpreted by adherence to written law, with whatever variations were considered acceptable in exigencies like the lynching of three murderers whose crimes did not require trials.

Jawn trooped back to bed.

Elrey did the same, up at the hotel, but he had a fitful and troubled rest. In the morning he lay a while with both arms behind his head. He had awakened with a disagreeable thought: Was he going to do his utmost to find the lynchers and jail them, hold them for trial, not because they had taken his prisoners out and hanged them, but because he had neglected to lock the roadway door, and because what they had done, while it may not have been in actual defiance of his authority, certainly reflected against him as a lawman sworn to perform the duties of his office, which included hunting down and arresting lynchers.

He had a late breakfast; the cafe was empty except for Amos Sanchez and the surly, slovenly, cafeman. They had been conversing in Spanish until Elrey walked in, then became silent. The cafeman said nothing to Elrey, he merely raised his eyebrows. Elrey gave his order and after the cafeman had departed he turned and smiled at Amos Sanchez, who smiled back from an otherwise closed face. Sanchez spoke first.

'And now it is finished.'

Elrey considered his reply, aware that whatever he said would spread, not only through Mex town, but through gringo town.

'The law,' he said, and saw Sanchez's closed look deepen. He started over. 'Amos, they deserved it, but suppose someone made up some bad story about you that got you arrested. A real bad story, the kind that'd get you lynched?'

The lanky Mexican made a thin smile. 'Suppose cows could fly, Elrey? It would be hard to get milk, eh? Or suppose they was put on trial and was turned loose? Or suppose — '

The cafeman arrived with Elrey's platter and interrupted to speak gruffly, sullenly. 'Constable, anywhere I ever lived them kind got shot or hanged. The law's fine; folks got to have laws, but what happened was decided by real law, not no book law.'

Elrey attacked his breakfast. He had not been aware of his hunger until the platter was in front of him. Sanchez chose this time to pay for his meal and depart. The cafeman, in an argumentative frame of mind, leaned on his pie table across from Elrey, watched the constable eat for a while, then bluntly said, 'They had it comin' an' as far I know folks are agreed about that, so what's the sense of keepin' it stirred up?'

Elrey did not respond. He finished his meal, put silver coins beside the platter, gave look for look with the cafeman, then walked through pleasantly cool morning sunlight to his office.

He did not notice that high mistiness had evaporated, suggesting there would be no rain after all.

When he returned to the roadway an hour or so later there was a wagon parked out yonder where three

211

townsmen were lowering the corpses from the cross member. He watched from the repaired overhang across the road in front of the general store. The proprietor came out wearing his flour-sack apron and black cotton sleeve protectors which reached from the wrist to the elbow. He sniffed and said, 'You wonderin' who sent 'em out there, Constable?'

'Yeah.'

'I did. That's hell of a sight for passengers on stages to see on their way to Coyanosa. Bad for the town. Bad for business. Anyway, hot as it is . . . '

Elrey watched the last dead man being lowered before the three men out yonder talked up the team and turned the wagon toward town. While watching this he said, 'You arrange for the burial too?'

'Yep. I didn't hear anyone else offerin' to. Diggers is already out at the graveyard.' The storekeeper sniffed. 'Cost me three dollars for them boys to fetch the bodies back and haul them up where the diggers will be waiting to drop them in an' close the graves. That's a week's wages for a lot of men, Constable.'

Elrey turned, studied the bird-like sniffing man for a moment then wagged his head. This townsman would never have got involved with a lynching.

He strolled down to the smithy where the blacksmith was hard pressed since he no longer had a helper, and he was not in a mood for conversation so, although he greeted Elrey, he went right on pumping his bellows.

Since it was impossible to have any kind of a discussion until that noise subsided, Elrey patiently leaned in the doorway.

Eventually the blacksmith, with whom Elrey had been friends for a long time, sighed and straightened up after warping cherry-coloured steel over a big anvil, shoved the steel back into the forge, made no move to pump the bellows and said, 'I know. I expected you'd be upset. Elrey, it had nothing to do with you. Folks are satisfied you're a good lawman.'

'But not good enough to bring them to trial, though.'

The blacksmith turned his steel bar in the forge before replying. 'I just told you folks respect you as a good lawman.'

Elrey continued to lean. 'Who did it?'

The blacksmith made a crooked smile. 'I work hard. A man at my trade don't stay up at night. He eats supper, washes off an' beds down. I don't know who done it, an' that's the truth. I was maybe the last man in town to see 'em hangin' out there in the morning. So help me.'

Before Elrey could speak the blacksmith pulled the cherry-red bar from the coals, handled it to the anvil and beat it, first on one side then on the other side, tapping the anvil with his hammer between strikes.

Elrey walked thoughtfully northward as far as the way-station. Pat Cullough was in his office, where it was blessedly cool against the rising morning heat.

He greeted Elrey with a gesture toward a chair and beat the constable to the punch by asking if Elrey had any idea who took his prisoners out yonder and hanged them.

Another time Elrey might have been tickled, but not this time. 'I thought you might know, Pat.'

Cullough looked shocked. 'Why would I know?'

'You were in town. They couldn't have done it without noise, could they?'

Cullough's surprise passed. He leaned on his untidy desk. 'Did you look close at them, Elrey?'

'On my horse when I came back to town. It was sort of dark. Why?'

'I don't think there was any noise. They was hauled out — '

'Pat, men who are scairt peeless and know they're goin' to get hung, make noise; they fight, they holler . . . '

'You didn't look close at them . . . They had rags tied over their mouths. They couldn't make a sound.

215

As for fightin', what could three men do against twice or three times that many other men?'

Elrey gazed thoughtfully at the other man. He had not heard of the dead men being gagged before, but then he had not heard much in the way of details from anyone.

'You saw them up close, Pat?'

'Elrey, it was my yardmen the storekeeper hired along with one of my wagons to go out there an' cut them down. No, I didn't see 'em close. My yardmen told me they'd been gagged with their own bandanas.'

Elrey sighed again during a discussion of the lynching. He had briefly thought he might have found someone who knew about the lynching, possibly a participant.

When he got back to the jailhouse Father Cross was waiting. As Elrey looked at his visitor he wondered for the hundredth time why priests wore those heavy, scratchy woollen habits during the heat. Someday he would ask, but today he nodded, put his hat aside and went to the desk before the priest spoke.

'Last night Chief Baca visited me. It was late, I am closing the chapel after prayers. He was waiting on a bench out back. When I came out he said, 'Sit down, Father. I have something for you.'

The priest paused and Elrey waited.

'He handed me a small leather pouch, and walked away, I think in the direction of the widow Bohorquez's house.'

Elrey was not interested in where Baca had gone. He leaned forward on the desk. 'The pouch, Father . . . ?'

'It held gold coins. I counted them in the morning.'

'How much?'

'Elrey, they told me my bulls would bring five dollars a head.'

'How much, Father?'

'Well for as many bulls as I had the price would have been — '

'Father, *how much*!'

'Three hundred dollars.'

Elrey let his gaze wander then brought it back. 'Did Chief say where the money came from?'

'No. Only that he had something for me. But you know Chief works for Dodge Plummer.'

Elrey's gaze wandered again. Dodge had done what he had mentioned to Elrey. He had gone among the cowmen and taken up a collection. He had undoubtedly continued to collect money even after he had the amount those fighting bulls would have brought from a buyer.

Father Cross said, 'The Lord taketh away and He giveth.'

Elrey almost smiled. It had been re-worded to fit the situation. 'Yes he does, Father. He also got you off the hook about those bulls.'

'I'm sorry they had to die that way, Elrey.' The priest arose. 'The carpenter has made a monument to the people killed . . . Don't you think he should have mentioned the real saviours of

Coyanosa, my longhorn bulls?'

Elrey smiled after the priest had departed. He liked the idea of commemorating the real saviours of the town. Across the headboard the carpenter should carve simply something like: To The Memory Of The Bulls Of Coyanosa. At the first opportunity he would mention that to the town council, but right now he had something else on his mind. It was too late in the day to do anything about it, but tomorrow before daylight . . .

13

The Hand of Fate

His plans for the following day were interrupted by the arrival in mid-morning of Feliciano Cortez. He had one rider with him who was left outside as Cortez entered the jailhouse office tugging off his gloves.

He and Elrey Austin were more nearly acquaintances than friends. Cortez had inherited a huge grant of land which, unlike most old Spanish and Mexican grants, had not been challenged by Yanqui authorities after the disastrous war with Mexico which had resulted in US acquisition of all the southwest.

Cortez was a large man, lighter than most natives, with eyes and hair as black as obsidian. He was wealthy and had a large family.

This morning as he shoved his hat back before sitting down he had the look of a man who had glimpsed Purgatory. His usual assertiveness was lacking as he said, 'Dodge told me the bulls are gone.'

Elrey nodded. 'As far as anyone knows right now.'

Cortez seemed to have scarcely heard. He fixed his dark gaze on something beyond the back wall as he also said he had contributed to Dodge Plummer's fund for the priest's reimbursement.

Elrey leaned back waiting and watching. There was more on the mind of Feliciano Cortez than the longhorn bulls.

He turned slowly to regard the constable. 'There is nothing left of the Mesa place. Dodge buried everyone. The buildings were burned to the ground.'

Elrey made an interjection because there was something left. 'Jeff's cattle and horses,' he said.

Cortez again seemed not to have heard. 'I went over there. I've seen other raids but nothing like this one. They must have caught Jeff and his people unprepared.'

Elrey nodded. Dodge had told him pretty much the same story.

Cortez blew out a shallow breath. 'Elrey, you'd have to see it to believe it. Worse than Apaches. Worse than anything you can imagine . . . Mesa's yard was only two miles from my headquarters.'

'You didn't hear gunfire, Felix?'

Cortez shook his head slowly. 'I was miles out with the riders. My wife and children were visiting her family over near Deloroso, for which I thank God.'

Cortez was noticeably shaken.

'They left tracks across the north-westerly part of my range on their way to the Mesa place. They could just as easily have attacked my place . . . My rangeboss says they probably had a scout out who saw the yard, found no one out there so they ran on over to the

Mesa place.' Cortez looked steadily at Elrey. 'I gave a hundred dollars for the priest.'

Elrey understood. 'Not for the bulls.'

'Well, no; for grateful prayers to God for sparing my family. But I rode in this morning to see the priest too. I want him to be sure to burn a hundred candles and say prayers of gratitude for a week, every morning.'

Cortez's expression changed slightly as he continued to address the constable. 'I heard what happened to your prisoners. If I knew who hanged them I would give them my thanks and some money. Who were they?'

Elrey shrugged. 'I don't know. Everyone I've talked to around town swears they knew nothing until they saw the corpses dangling out yonder.'

Cortez thought about that, then arose to depart as he said, 'Whoever they were I owe them. If you find out I'd like to know.'

Elrey arose behind his desk. 'If I find out,' he drily said, 'you'll hear about it.'

Maybe the tone rather than the words caused Cortez to linger gazing at the constable. 'Listen to me,' he quietly said. 'This is something those men deserved. Those who hanged them punished those men exactly as they deserved. Maybe the law would have done it, maybe not. I very much doubt it. What could have happened to my family, for which I give thanks did not happen, and what did happen elsewhere, right here in town . . . Elrey, I don't think you understand.'

Elrey said he understood perfectly. He did not say the law had been violated. There was no point in mentioning that to a man whose life had narrowly missed being devastated. But he did say he intended to find out who the lynchers were, and Cortez stood in the doorway regarding him a long moment before closing the door after himself.

Later, when he would still have time to do what he had intended to do today, he was out back cuffing a horse before saddling it, when a tall, leathery-faced man came around the side of the jailhouse, leaned to watch and said, 'My name is Charles Billings. Commanding officer at the Antelope Valley army post outside Guadalupe up north. Are you Constable Austin?'

Elrey finished the cuffing, tossed the comb and brush into a box and confirmed who he was. He also had a premonition that what he had planned to do today, was destined not to be done. Today anyway.

Billings's uniform was faded, rumpled and sweat-stained. He was a ruddy man of solid heft and thoughtful bearing. He had heard of the lynchings and was disappointed because he had come down to Coyanosa to take the prisoners back up north for a military trial.

New Mexico was a territory, not a state. The army had jurisdiction in areas it administrated. Captain Billings lighted a thin, dark cigar as he told Elrey of a fruitless hunt for the renegades. As he puffed up a fragrant head of smoke he also said, 'Damndest thing I ever heard, wild bulls fighting those renegades. I doubt they'll believe my report in Washington.'

Elrey resignedly took the officer into the cool office. Only then did the officer mention the lynching. Elrey repeated what he had told others. When he found out who had taken the prisoners out of his jailhouse and hanged them, he would bring them in and lock them up.

Captain Billings smoked, regarded the ash tip of his stogie and spoke in a measured, slow manner. 'Constable, those renegades marched us ragged. Even after some of us acquired horses they still out-ran us. They changed course five times. We finally lost them when they rode all night and we had to stop.' Captain Billings leaned to tip ash into the metal tray on Elrey's desk. 'Last night I camped near a burned out ranch with fresh graves.'

'The Mesa place,' Elrey said.

The officer nodded. 'It was not a fight, Constable, it was a wanton massacre.'

Elrey nodded about that. He was curious about something. 'Did they steal horses as they went along? Otherwise how — ?'

'Stole horses every place they found them, mostly running free on the range. We could not do that; what horses we eventually acquired we got ranchers to loan us.' The officer made a thin smile. 'They were glad to put us a-horseback, they knew about the renegades. But my column consisted of two companies. We could not get that many horses. We got fifty head, but every time we had to halt the renegades kept moving.'

Captain Billings placed his cigar stub in the tin tray where it would die a normal death. He returned to his earlier topic. He was a slow-speaking man careful with words, something he had no doubt learned after half a lifetime in uniform.

'Mister Austin, if we had taken your

prisoners back up north we would have tried and hanged them. Military courts have one judgement to pass on men like that.' The officer smiled a little. 'Lynching is certainly against military as well as civilian law.'

Elrey nodded, suspecting where this discussion was going.

Captain Billings flicked a grey ash off his knee. 'If you find the lynchers, Mister Austin, they will be subject to military law.' He raised his head to look steadily at the constable. 'Are you familiar with military law?'

Elrey was not and shook his head.

The officer leaned back in his chair. 'Soldiers and citizens alike are entitled under our law to defend their lives by any available means.'

Elrey said, 'They took them out of here and hanged them at a corral north of town. It was not a matter of self — '

'Mister Austin, they were the worst kind of murderers. Suppose they had broken out of your jailhouse; they would have found guns and killed people who got in their way.'

Elrey stared uneasily at the captain, who returned the gaze with one just as direct, but less indignant, more calm and what seemed to be an unwavering regard of the man at the desk.

Elrey relaxed, leaned on the desk with clasped hands. 'And if I find the lynchers?'

'Constable, I'm older than you, I've spent most of my life on the frontier, if you identify the lynchers . . . Say nothing to them and don't send me notice up at Guadalupe.'

'You believe lynching is right?'

'Mister Austin, I believe — I *know* — someday after you and I are dust, book-law will govern out here. Right now our situation is simply too few soldiers for the size of the area to be patrolled, and town lawmen like you whose authority actually does not go beyond your town limits, which leaves two judges to care for crimes neither you nor I can handle because we either have not the authority or the men — Judge Colt and Judge Hemp.'

The captain arose. He was a handsome man in a rugged way. He smiled and offered a big hand. Elrey arose, shook the hand and smiled back.

After the officer left Elrey moved to a window and watched him cross the road, pick up his companion in blue and turn northward in the direction of Jawn Kelly's saloon.

Elrey threw up his hands. It was too late to do what he had planned. He sat at the desk, cocked back his chair and was sitting like that with both hands behind his head when Father Cross entered, flushed and sweaty, outside the day was boiling hot.

As the priest nodded and went to the olla for a drink, Elrey asked a question. 'Father, it's over a hundred out there. No one in his right mind wears heavy wool when it's this hot.'

The little priest mopped off sweat and sank down on a bench. 'It is our scourge,' he replied, and before Elrey could press this subject, he also said,

'Feliciano Cortez came to the mission.'

Elrey was not surprised. 'We talked this morning.'

'He gave me money for a hundred candles and more money for the mission if I would pray his thanks to God.' Father Cross looked sardonic about this. 'Of course I agreed, but I had to ask why he didn't do it himself, why he didn't put his family in a wagon and visit the mission some Sunday. Even if they left early they could still arrive there by late Mass.'

'What did he say?'

'He promised to do that next Sunday.' The priest gave a slight shrug. 'In my experience the distance someone lives from the mission, the more miles they have to reflect on reasons for not making such a trip.' Father Cross smiled. 'Fortunately God has heard all the excuses for over a thousand years. He has to be a forgiving God, doesn't he? Otherwise his disposition as well as his faith in humanity would have soured him long ago, eh?'

Elrey laughed.

It was mid-afternoon when Elrey got up to Jawn Kelly's establishment, and as he had expected, during the hottest time of the day the saloon was empty except for Jawn Kelly, who was sound asleep in a cocked-back chair with a scattering of ancient newspaper where it had fallen from his hands.

Elrey leaned on the bar as one of Jawn Kelly's surprisingly blue eyes opened and swiveled around to behold the constable.

He yawned mightily, rocked the chair down off the wall and went behind his bar where he wordlessly drew off two glasses of tepid beer, placed one in front of the constable and held the other one as he said, 'Did you know there were soldiers in town?'

Elrey drank half his beer before replying. 'Yeah. I talked to the officer. He's from the post up at Guadalupe.'

'He's a long way from home. What did he want?'

Elrey considered the remaining beer

in his glass before answering. 'He wanted the prisoners.'

'And you told him?'

'He already knew,' Elrey replied and drained the glass before pushing it away. 'He explained military law to me.'

Jawn's scowl formed slowly. 'What does that mean?'

'I think it means that when someone is dead the military has no more interest in them.'

Jawn's face cleared. 'Well, who has?'

Elrey regarded his old friend. 'No one, I expect. They sure can't be brought back an' hanged again, can they?'

Jawn Kelly leaned and stared steadily across the bar. He knew Elrey Austin as well as anyone did in Coyanosa. He sighed and rolled his eyes skyward. 'But you got a bone in your teeth an' don't aim to let go.'

Elrey did not reply. He placed a coin beside his empty glass and walked out of the cool saloon into the full fury of late-day heat.

He did not return to the jailhouse, but went up to his room at the hotel, draped a blanket over the window and bedded down.

It had been siesta time since high noon but that was not what had decided him to sleep away the hot time of day. He had missed sleep lately and even after returning from Oak Canyon he had not slept well.

Now he did. He intended to leave Coyanosa before first light in the morning. It was a long ride to his destination and a long ride back. For all he knew when he got out there he might be delayed for hours. For that reason he slept soundly, which he could not have done if the old hotel hadn't once been a Mexican barracks and had mud walls three feet thick. It never got hot in his room and in winter it never got really cold.

He missed supper, something which did not bother him, but in the pre-dawn morning chill and darkness he saw the light in the cafe and although the door was locked, he banged on it until the disagreeable proprietor opened the door wearing a frown, ready to snarl until he saw who his first customer was, then, as he shuffled back toward his cooking area he said, 'My paw told me once any man who arises before daylight's got a bad conscience. Did you know there was a couple of soldiers in town?'

Elrey knew. 'What is for breakfast?'

'Fat pork, fried spuds an' coffee.'

'Yeah I knew there was soldiers in town. Two of 'em.'

'What you reckon they're here for?'

Elrey twisted as someone else walked in out of the darkness. It was Chief Baca. Elrey nodded and suppressed his surprise. Baca yelled at the cafeman, who growled a response, then Chief turned toward Elrey with a quizzical expression. 'You couldn't sleep?'

Elrey's reply was casual. 'Got some riding to do today.'

When their platters arrived the cafeman put a sly, knowing smile upon

Chief Baca. Before he could make one of his snide remarks Chief pointed a rigid finger at him. The cafeman slunk back to his cooking area.

Baca winked at Elrey and went to work on his meal. He ate fast because he too had a long ride ahead and he did not want to reach the yard after the work had been parcelled out and everyone was gone.

Elrey took a chance. 'Why don't you just get a job in town?'

Baca chewed a long time, swallowed then answered in a voice that would not carry to the cooking area. 'That's the second time I been asked that in the last twenty-four hours.'

'Well?'

Baca continued to eat for a while before coming up with an answer, then it was a question instead of a statement. 'Elrey, have you ever been married?'

'Married? No, never have.'

'I've heard they eat a lot, need new clothes every now'n then, and get as cranky as a horsing mare about every month or so.'

Elrey had no answer to any of that. But he did say men got married, even in the Coyanosa country, every once in a while and as far as he knew, they seemed to do well enough, and for a fact those who were skinny as snakes from batching, began to put on weight, get their hair cut regularly and wore clean shirts.

Chief listened and ate, said no more on the subject until after Elrey departed and the cafeman came along to make another attempt at being sly. This time Chief was standing up counting silver coins to be placed beside his dish, and after the cafeman leered and made a remark, Chief finished putting the silver down, straightened back, drew his sixgun, cocked it and smiled.

He did not say a word. Neither did the slovenly cafeman. Not then and not later.

14

End of the Trail

It was a beautiful morning. They all were between first light and forenoon, even for several hours after the sun arrived.

Elrey was in no hurry because somewhere up ahead was Chief Baca and if he had wanted to ride with him he would have mentioned it back at the cafe.

He was riding the sorrel again. It was rested and right up there in the bit, so much so in fact that when they came too close to a meadow lark's nest and the bird exploded upwards nearby, the sorrel horse shied like a colt, for which he was roundly cursed as Elrey got him lined out again in the correct direction.

Elrey did not see Chief Baca. He had probably left town earlier, or more likely, he had loped most of the way, but for whatever reason Elrey did not see him so the entire world that he could see was out there just for his pleasure.

The distance was not great but neither was it insignificant. None of the ranches were close to Coyanosa even though several of them owned the range that reached to the outskirts of town.

When Elrey had the Plummer yard in sight with its unkempt old trees and grey-weathered sturdy buildings a dog barked but no one was in the yard until he came close enough to reach tree-shade, then someone who had evidently been watching him for some time, emerged from around beside the bunkhouse.

It was the chore-boy, the same lithe young Mexican lad whom Dodge Plummer had brought to town at the height of the renegade scare.

Elrey called a greeting in Spanish. The lad replied without making any move to approach the man tying his sorrel horse.

Elrey had a feeling of being nearly alone. No rider appeared nor did Dodge who ordinarily came out onto the long porch of the main-house when visitors arrived.

Elrey leaned on the tie rack regarding the chore-boy. 'Anyone around?' he asked.

The youth shook his head and gestured northwesterly. 'Out there.'

Elrey sighed. 'How long ago did they leave?'

'Not long, a little while before you came.'

Elrey unlooped his reins, swung over leather and left the yard in a slow lope, his idea being to overtake Dodge and his riders who would be riding at a walk.

He was lucky. With a vast expanse of land to consider and shod-horse tracks in all directions, if someone hadn't fired a gun he would have had trouble finding them.

There was just one shot. It came

from the more northerly direction than westerly.

He boosted the sorrel over into a lope and rocketed along until he saw them in the distance. It looked like the entire crew. They were riding, but obviously they had stopped for a while, otherwise they would have been farther along. One of them had shot a rattlesnake.

They were beginning to scatter wide, the way riders did who were making a sweep for cattle, when someone looked back, saw Elrey coming, and raised the yell until all the others stopped and turned to watch.

Elrey recognised Dodge by his slouched position in the saddle, the way he sat up there, gloved hands loose on the horn. He also recognised Chief Baca and Boss Cleaver. The others he knew by sight, not by name.

When he hauled down to a walk from a few yards out, the sorrel hiked along with swinging reins as the men eyed each other.

When Elrey was close enough Dodge

said, 'You must've got up before breakfast.'

Elrey smiled. It was an old joke. He nodded to Baca who showed none of the surprise he might have shown to see Elrey out here when they could have made the ride together.

Boss Cleaver had a dark expression. Lately, every time he'd met the Coyanosa constable it had meant some kind of damned involvement that kept him from his work.

Dodge was gazing woodenly at Elrey, waiting. Elrey did not keep him waiting long. He said, 'I know you got work to do, but I'd like to talk to you alone for a few minutes.'

Dodge spat amber, dragged a glove across his mouth and spoke to his riders without taking his eyes off Elrey. 'Go ahead, boys. You know where they should be. I'll catch up when I can.'

The rangemen were expressionless. They were also reluctant to leave their employer because the constable clearly had something in mind that might mean problems.

Dodge turned, scowled at his range-boss. Boss Cleaver reined around frowning and jerked his head. The riders rode away scattering again to make their sweep.

Dodge swung to the ground and squatted holding one split rein. His face was blank, his habitually narrowed eyes never left Elrey who also dismounted.

There were no trees close by but as yet the morning was still cool.

Elrey began softly. 'When you come to town after the raid, after you'd buried Jeff Mesa and the others out yonder, you told me you had to get back to the ranch.'

'That's right; over in front of the store it was. What of it?'

'Dodge, you didn't even stop at the saloon on your way out of town.'

The old man's narrowed eyes were stone-steady. 'Nope, we didn't stop on the way out. I know it's the custom, but we'd already had a drink when we come into town, before I come down an' talked to you.'

Elrey smiled a little returning the older man's look eye for eye. 'You got a rider named Jack Buford?'

'Yes. You know that.'

'Yeah. Dodge, Jack Buford told Jawn Kelly about a survivor of the raid hiding in Oak Canyon.'

This time the old stockman spat amber and said nothing.

Elrey held his small, mirthless smile giving stare for stare with Dodge Plummer. 'Jawn came down to the jailhouse to tell me. You know the rest, don't you?'

'You went out there?'

Elrey put forth something he did not know for a fact but which he believed. 'Yeah, I went out there, an' you know I did.'

Again the older man said nothing. This time he did not expectorate, he stared steadily at the younger man opposite him.

'Dodge, you didn't ride back to the ranch, did you?'

Plummer spat and shifted a little, said nothing and for the first time let his gaze wander from the constable's face.

Elrey continued, from this point on saying things he could not prove. 'You rode out a ways and waited until you saw me leave town for Oak Canyon. Then you took your riders back, one of 'em used the darkness to jimmy the jailhouse door and go through to let the rest of you in from the alley.

'You gagged the prisoners and dragged them into the back alley. You took them north to the bull corral and hanged them from the cross piece above the gate. Then you rode home.'

Dodge Plummer arose stiffly, turned and leaned across the seat of his saddle looking westward. Elrey also arose. He stood watching Dodge Plummer with thumbs hooked in his shellbelt.

It was a long wait before the older man spoke without facing around. 'Whatever you figure to do, Elrey, it won't never work in gawd's green world.' Dodge finally faced around. 'Wasn't no one out there from town. No one saw — '

'I know that, Dodge. That's what set me to thinking, I talked to a lot of people. Every blessed one of them was surprised to see those fellers hangin' out there. So, if it wasn't someone from town . . .'

The old man jettisoned his cud and ran a sleeve across his mouth. 'You should have been at the Mesa place when we got over there. I'm a lot older'n you, I've seen what's left after In'ians finish. I never in my life saw anything like what those sons of bitches did at the Mesa place.'

Elrey remained silent.

'My conscience don't bother me at all, Elrey. To tell you the truth I wasn't sure you'd figure things out or not. An' I honestly didn't care if you did. When Chief come in about the time we saddlin' up this morning he told me there was soldiers in town. I expect you'd know more about that than he would, but whether they got some notion about arrestin' the lynchers, I don't care about that either, an' I'll tell you why: the army's shot and hung more renegades than I've ever seen. If that ain't enough, Elrey, there's not a soul in the Territory who'd set in judgment on us for what we done.' The older man spoke matter-of-factly, without defiance and without anger, and he smiled. 'You figured things out right well. I always said you was the best we've had an' I've seen 'em come an' go for a lot of years.'

As they faced one another Elrey gently wagged his head. 'Dodge, that's the way it once was, an' I'm not sayin' it was wrong, but — '

'But you're sayin' it was wrong the other night. Well, like the man said, Elrey, you go to your church an' I'll go to mine . . . You come out to arrest me an' haul me back to town?'

Elrey shook his head. 'Just to talk to you.'

The older man's shrewd, narrowed

eyes showed irony. 'Let me ask you a question, Elrey: Do you believe them sons of bitches shouldn't have been hanged? Now wait a minute. The army would have hung them. Any judge worth his salt would have sentenced them to be hung an' I expect you know it. Tell me flat out — do you think they shouldn't have been hung?'

Elrey's gaze at the older man was unwavering. It also had the barest hint of amusement when Elrey replied.

'They should have been hung. The soldier I talked to yesterday said pretty much what you just said. But there's a hell of a distance between lynching and legal hanging, Dodge.'

The older man snorted. 'Same hemp rope, Elrey, same threshin' around.' Dodge threw up his hands before speaking again. 'All right; we could stand here all day, so I'm goin' to offer you a trade. I'll let you handle 'em after this, an' if you do it proper, I'll leave it up to you no matter what.'

It was a lead-pipe cinch that was the

best Elrey was going to get from Dodge Plummer who did not have one iota of remorse in his stringy old carcass. He thought it was fair so he shoved out his hand.

Dodge pumped it and let go, as he turned to gather both reins along his horse's neck he said, 'I did feel sort of measly, sendin' you off on that wild goose chase.' Plummer rose up over leather before finishing it. 'On the other hand I sure didn't want to throw down on you an' lock you in your own jailhouse, that would be hard for a lawman to live down.'

Dodge lifted his left hand with the reins in it, winked and turned to boot his animal over into a lope heading north.

All the way back to Coyanosa Elrey went over what they had said to one another. By the time he was in the corral out behind the *juzgado* he had decided that Dodge Plummer was still his friend. He had also decided that after all Dodge had done for the priest and his dilapidated old mission, maybe the matter of lynching those worthless renegades really did not loom very large in comparison with other things.

He went up to Jawn Kelly's place. Because it was nearly nighttime and Jawn's regulars had been fed supper which permitted them time to visit the saloon for a nightcap, the place would be about as full as it ever was on a week-day night.

Jawn had customers along his bar and one card table had players around it, but the tone of the saloon was subdued.

Jawn caught Elrey's eye and jerked his head. They met at the southern-most curve of the bar without anyone close. Jawn said, 'Well; did you bring him in?'

Elrey frowned. 'Bring who in?'

'Dodge Plummer. It's been the talk of the town since someone saw you leave town before sunup ridin' toward the Plummer place.'

Elrey's eyes widened a little. 'Is that

why it was so quiet when I walked in tonight?'

'Yes . . . Did you?'

'No, I didn't bring him in.'

'Couldn't find him?'

'I found him.'

Jawn fidgetted. This was like pulling teeth. 'You found him an' he refused to let you fetch him back?'

Elrey reddened a little. 'I didn't go out there to bring him in. I went out there to talk to him . . . Jawn, you told me you didn't know a damned thing about that lynching!'

'I told you I didn't know they was hung out there until a couple of fellers come into the saloon who saw 'em dangling, an' that's the truth.'

Elrey leaned on the bar. 'You knew it was Plummer?'

'You didn't ask me that. You didn't ask anyone that.'

'How did you know?'

Jawn ignored impatient customers who were banging the bartop for service. 'Because Dodge rode out after his rider told me that story about someone bein' holed up in Oak Canyon. After you left town Pat Cullough was out back behind town an' saw a bunch of riders standing out a ways beside their horses watchin' you go.'

The customers were becoming increasingly demanding, Jawn pulled back off the bar and made one final statement. 'I told you to forget it.'

Elrey lingered at the saloon for a while then headed for his room to bed down. As he was shucking his boots it occurred to him that when everybody else is wrong and someone else is right, there had to be something out of whack with the feller who was right.

He fell asleep this night with none of the hauntings which had troubled his rest previous nights. He hadn't won and he hadn't lost, the lynched men were buried, the range troubles had been resolved, Father Cross got more money than he had expected to get, and Elrey Austin had learned that whatever the law stood for elsewhere, in the middle part of New Mexico it was not blind, but it might as well have been, because in the Coyanosa country it thought with its heart.

THE END

We do hope that you have enjoyed reading this large print book.

Did you know that all of our titles are available for purchase?

We publish a wide range of high quality large print books including:
Romances, Mysteries, Classics, General Fiction, Non Fiction and Westerns.

Special interest titles available in large print are:
The Little Oxford Dictionary Music Book, Song Book Hymn Book, Service Book

Also available from us courtesy of Oxford University Press:
Young Readers' Dictionary (large print edition) Young Readers' Thesaurus (large print edition)

For further information or a free brochure, please contact us at:
Ulverscroft Large Print Books Ltd., The Green, Bradgate Road, Anstey, Leicester, LE7 7FU, England. Tel: (00 44) **0116 236 4325 Fax:** (00 44) **0116 234 0205**

The stage robbery had been accomplished by an old woman. Twine Fourch had never heard of a female being a highway robber before. He followed the trail all the way to a dilapidated log cabin up Stone Mountain. What happened after that no one could believe even after townsmen from Jefferson found the old log house and the skeletal dying old woman. But before the mystery could be solved there would be two unnecessary killings, a bizarre suicide and a lynching.

GUNS OF THE GAMBLER

M. Duggan

Destitute gambler Ben Crow arrives in Mallory keen to claim his inheritance, only to discover that rancher Edward Bacon has other ideas. Set up by Miss Dorothy, who had fooled him completely, Ben finds himself dangling on the end of a rope. Saved from death, Ben sets off in pursuit of Miss Dorothy, determined upon retribution. However, his quest for vengeance turns into a rescue mission when she is kidnapped by a crazy man-burning bandit.

SIDEWINDER

John Dyson

All Flynn wants is to be Marshal of Tucson, but he is framed by the territory's richest rancher, Frank Buchanan, and thrown into Yuma prison. Five years later Flynn comes out, intent on clearing his name and burning for vengeance. Fists thud, knives flash and bullets fly as he rides both sides of the law and participates in kidnapping and double-dealing. He is once again arrested for a murder of which he is innocent. Can he escape the noose a second time?

THE BLOODING OF JETHRO

Frank Fields

When Jethro Smith's family is murdered by outlaws, vengeance is the one thing on his mind. He meets the brother of one of the murderers, who attempts to exploit Jethro's grudge in the pursuit of his own vendetta. The local preacher, formerly a sheriff, teaches Jethro how to use a gun. With his new-found skills, Jethro and his somewhat unwelcome friend pit themselves against seemingly impossible odds. Whatever the outcome lead would surely fly.